I0623179

THE OFFICE SPY

A REX & EDDIE MYSTERY

SEAN CAMERON

DAPPER FOX
PUBLISHING

Cover Design: Anthony S. Hales

ISBN-13: 978-1-946215-03-1

ONE

"Corporate espionage," Rex said with a grin stretched across his face. "Espionage," he repeated, enjoying every syllable.

He took a deep breath through his nose as if he smelled something sweet. Unfortunately for him, the nearby Cloisterham River was notorious for its brown murkiness and stench. Rex coughed up the ghastly odour that the morning tide had brought in.

Eddie peered up at the six-storey building made of thin layers of yellow brick and tinted black windows. He turned to Rex. "I'm partial to the word 'corporate' myself."

Rex narrowed his eyes enough to let his round-framed glasses slide a little down his nose. "That's a boring word. Why do you like that?"

"Because it means we get paid, and we can finally call ourselves *professional* detectives. Corporations have money. Money means a paying client. No rewards, no IOUs, just straight-up billable hours; expenses even. This case could be the making of us."

The pair walked across the riverside office's car park and up the concrete steps to the building's entrance.

Rex held the door open. "We should make Milton Miles Investigations into a corporation, then we'd have money too."

Eddie scoffed as he passed through the doorway. "It doesn't work like that."

Inside, the dingy reception walls were covered in blue felt. The repetitive pattern on the floor tiles gave away it was fake marble. A third of the ceiling's fluorescent bulbs were dead, which lit the security guard's desk like an eccentric art installation.

A tubby-faced man in his early thirties sat at the desk, facing a stack of grey security monitors.

"We're pest control, here for Sparklefeet Industries," Eddie said.

"It's on the third floor." The security guard pushed a clipboard along the desk. "Sign in."

Rex eagerly wrote both their names down while Eddie pushed the call button for the elevator. As they got into the lift, Eddie examined their brown, zip-up jumpsuits in the mirrored walls. On an ordinary day, both looked younger than their twenty-eight years. Eddie had hoped dressing up in the attire of a working man would make him more manly; instead, the pair looked like skinny twelve-year-olds in Daddy's work clothes.

The brown collar itched the back of Eddie's neck. When he tried to pull the collar away, he caused the back of the jumpsuit to ride up between his buttocks. He glowered at Rex, who was several inches taller than Eddie, yet comfortable in his slightly baggy jumpsuit.

"What?" Rex asked. "I think the costumes are great."

"They're called disguises, not costumes." Eddie turned

to give Rex the cold shoulder, but the elevator's mirrored walls showed an endless line of confused Rexs.

"You don't like them?" Rex's reflection said.

Eddie spun to the real Rex and pointed at the stitched-in badge on Rex's left breast pocket. On the badge, below an embossed image of a cartoon beetle, were the words 'Milton Miles Exterminations.'

"You put our surnames on the jumpsuits."

"What was I supposed to put?"

"I don't know, AAA Exterminators, something like that."

"That name was taken. I checked the phone book."

"Now if they do an online search, they'll find our detective agency is also called Milton Miles Investigations."

"We have a website?"

Eddie gritted his teeth. "Yes, we do." He sighed and prodded Rex's jumpsuit logo. "And was the slogan necessary?"

Rex rolled his eyes. "What's wrong with the slogan?"

"'If you've got pests, we're the bests.' 'Bests' isn't even a word."

"Do you want to make new ones?"

Eddie calmed. "We can't claim expenses for two sets of uniforms, we'd look like amateurs."

He checked himself in the mirror wall and adjusted his hair using his fingers as a comb. Eddie always had the same, neat haircut: short back and sides with an inch on top. As a rule, he never allowed the top to grow more than three inches, but two and a half was the preferable cut-off point. Due to budget issues, Eddie's hair was dangerously close to the three-inch mark. In contrast to Rex's shaggy hairdo, he still appeared neat, but Eddie still shamefully tucked the sides behind his ears as he straightened up.

The elevator pinged as the doors opened. Rex and

Eddie passed through the third-floor hallway to Sparklefeet Inc's office entrance.

A spritely young woman in her mid-twenties approached. She had golden blonde hair, black-framed glasses, a low-cut white shirt, and a tight black skirt. Her face was pretty and triangular, which accentuated her ruby lips. As her high heels clopped towards them, she extended a hand. Eddie's heart raced a little as she arrived.

"Welcome to Sparklefeet Inc, I'm Bessie."

Eddie shook her hand. "Eddie Miles, Milton Miles Investigations."

"And you must be Rex Milton."

Rex nodded. "Yes, I'm his partner."

"Business partner," Eddie added.

Her polite smile lingered. "Follow me."

Bessie walked them through the sparse office. A dozen or so glum employees were scattered around the rows of grey desks divided by worn-out partition walls.

The pair followed Bessie towards a big corner office with glass walls. Inside, a trim man with designer stubble and premature grey hair stood over a conference speaker. The sign on the door read, 'Dorian West, CEO of Sparklefeet Inc.'

Bessie knocked.

"Enter," said a crisp, deep voice inside.

The pair followed Bessie inside.

"So, listen guys. I've got to go," Dorian said into the conference speaker. "If you can get those numbers down by ten percent, then I'm in. Otherwise, no deal. Okay?"

He slammed his thumb on the red button, ending the call before there was a response. Dorian looked up and smiled as if he were a model in a toothpaste advert. Handsome and well-manicured, he could advertise anything: hair, spray tan, contacts, moisturiser, anything.

"Rex and Eddie, right?"

Dorian paraded around his broad, curved executive desk and offered a firm handshake. Eddie obliged, finding Dorian's hand overly forceful. Rex followed and shook back with as much gusto.

"I'm glad you gentlemen are here. We're taking a kicking from this spy character." Dorian gracefully lowered into his office chair, its large, black, plastic backrest made the chair seem like an ergonomic throne. "How long will it take?"

"Uh, well … there's lots to consider," Eddie said. "We need to search for surveillance equipment in phones, security cameras, sweep for secret microphones, we have to check everything with our detectors."

Dorian nodded as he interlocked his fingers. "Sounds thorough. And you said on the phone you charge thirty-pounds an hour?"

Eddie swallowed. "Yes."

"And it would take hours," Rex said.

"How many hours?"

Eddie bared his teeth at Rex, Rex shut his mouth.

"Tens of hours?" Eddie said, worried saying days sounded too much. "For the preliminary search."

"Excellent."

Eddie smiled for a brief second. Then he frowned, wondering if he under-bid. "Well, yes. But first, Mr West—"

"Dorian, please."

"Dorian, what makes you think you have a spy?"

"We sell a liquid solution for cleaning shoes, especially trainers, running shoes, that sort of thing. With our solution, even the whitest trainers can be returned to their former glory. I announced a strategy to the staff, and our rivals, Klean Loafers, beat us to it. Now our stock prices have plummeted."

Eddie nodded. "Tell me about Klean Loafers."

"It's run by Ash Haynes, a man that used to work for me. Ash and I had disagreements, so we parted ways. He set up a company six months ago that ripped off my formula."

"Right, so can you sue him?"

"The formula is a secret. If I sue, I'd have to show that the formula is the same by giving away my ingredients, then anyone can copy us."

"But Ash knows the formula?"

"In the beginning, he helped me batch-make the soap in my mother's bathtub. Now I have a factory, an office, and salespeople at major shopping centres in Kent, Essex, and Surrey."

Rex smiled. "That's impressive."

"Ash is taking over. I don't have exclusivity with the shopping centres, so we have to directly compete with him. I tried to implement a new price, a new sales strategy, but he does the exact same thing faster than us."

Rex scratched his chin. "Like what?"

"I wanted to give away a second brush in the cleaning pack. That way we gave more value. We ordered the brushes and all of a sudden, Klean Loafers did it before us. How do I compete with that?"

"Three brushes?" Rex asked.

"What are they gonna do with three brushes? That's stupid. You do two brushes and a washcloth. Klean Loafers beat us to that as well."

Ashamed, Rex stared down at his feet.

"Now, gentleman," Dorian waved his lusciously thick hair away from his face, "I've got to make some calls. Find the leak, and I will pay you handsomely."

"We get paid by the hour though, right?" Eddie blurted.

Dorian paused. "Of course. I meant I'll throw in a little bonus."

Eddie's nervousness settled.

"A handsome bonus," Rex said.

Dorian snapped his fingers. "I like him. Pays attention to the details. That's important." He stood and approached the pair. "As requested, Bessie informed the staff you're pest exterminators doing a routine inspection. No one knows you're here to find our spy." Having circled the pair, he patted them on the back. "Well, men, do you need anything from me?"

"We just … uh, we spoke on the phone about expenses for the uniforms."

Dorian nodded. "See Bessie about the petty cash."

Bessie opened her desk drawer and pulled out a little locked metal box. As she unlocked and opened it, Rex and Eddie leaned closer to peek inside, as if it was buried treasure. Their shadows blocked her light. She looked up at the pair with a furrowed brow.

"Do you mind?"

They leaned back.

She counted through a short stack of twenty-pound notes. It was the most cash the two detectives had seen in a while.

Eddie smiled as he handed over a scrunched-up receipt. "Two hundred, please?"

"That's a bit expensive. Were the gold trim cuffs necessary?"

Eddie gave Rex a scornful look.

Rex sighed. "I didn't know we had a budget."

She rolled her eyes and placed the cash in Eddie's hand.

The pair walked around the office, wondering where to start.

"I like that box of money," Rex said. "What's it called?"

"Petty cash."

"We should have a petty cash."

"We're broke," Eddie said. "All our cash is petty."

In the middle of the open office, Rex lowered to the thin, grey carpet and placed his ear to the ground.

"Get up," Eddie muttered. " Rex! Up. Now."

Rex shuffled along on all fours and paused again.

Several office workers watched from their desks. Eddie dreaded the idea that someone would know him and think he'd actually become a pest exterminator. Rex waved at the audience without a care.

A large man in a blue suit with big arms, a wide neck, and a crew cut approached holding a cup of tea. He stopped at Rex's head. Rex noticed the man's black boots and glanced up at him.

The man sipped his tea. "So you found any bugs?"

Rex smiled. "That's currently under investigation—"

"Uh, inspection," Eddie said. "That's under *inspection*."

The man gulped from his mug. "I've got an ant problem at home, what's your website?"

"We don't have one," Eddie said.

"This is the twenty-first century. You need a website."

"Well, we work on a referral only basis."

"You're not gonna expand your business like that."

Eddie sneered.

"Sorry." The man offered his free hand. "Gary Allen, director of sales."

While Eddie shook Gary's massive hand, Rex climbed up onto an empty desk and stared at the ceiling. He prodded a polystyrene panel.

Gary paused the handshake to watch Rex jump on the desk. "You fellas want a ladder?"

Rex re-found his balance. "Yes, please."

Gary released Eddie's worn out hand and left.

With folded arms, Rex tilted his head at the ceiling.

"Please, get off the table," Eddie said.

Rex huffed and climbed down. "This isn't my kind of investigation. Don't you miss the excitement of a proper case?"

Eddie shook his head. "I'm not a fan of being chased by dangerous people. This is a steady paycheque, that makes it a proper case, a perfect case. If we do a professional job, I suspect we'll get a lot more cases like it."

Rex slumped, disappointed.

"So be careful what you say or do, we don't want anyone to know we aren't really pest control. We blow our cover, we blow the case."

After Gary returned with a ladder, Rex climbed to the ceiling and lifted the first panel. He popped his head into the hole.

Eddie held the ladder. "Anything suspicious?"

"Suspicious?" Gary asked as he swished the last of his tea around the mug.

Eddie shrugged. "You know, rat droppings and stuff."

"It's really dark," Rex said.

"Give me a go."

Rex came down, and Eddie climbed up into the ceiling hole, feeling self-conscious with Gary watching. With his head inside the dark ceiling, Eddie squinted, which didn't help him see. Instead, the squinting flared his nostrils and allowed enough dust in to set off a sneezing fit.

Eddie climbed down, his eyes welling up.

"Did you see anything?" Rex asked, paying little attention to Eddie's sinus troubles.

"No." Eddie searched his pockets for a tissue. Since the jumpsuit had multiple pockets, it took some time.

"You fellas need a light? I can bring you a torch. I'd have thought you'd have a torch."

Feeling unprepared and embarrassed, Eddie puffed his chest out. "Um, we do."

Gary pinned his chin back, confused by the hostility. "Why don't you use it?"

"Uh, the batteries ran out."

"I can give you some batteries. What size do they take?"

Eddie narrowed one eye. "Triple-A…?"

Gary nodded and walked off.

Eddie turned to Rex. "I need you to go to the shops and get a torch. One that takes triple-A batteries, okay?"

"With the petty cash?"

"Use the change from the jumpsuits."

Rex just stared.

"You spent all of it? On what?"

"I bought those hats and glasses to disguise our faces. We should give Bessie the receipt, and we'll have money again."

"We're not expensing those. You can't wear a trilby hat to hide the fact you're a detective; they're detective hats. Anyway, it would be weird with these uniforms. You'll have to take them back to the shop."

"They were on sale, no returns."

"Perfect," Eddie said. "One hour into the job and we're already losing money."

Gary returned with a camping lamp. "We're out of triple-A batteries, but will this do?"

Eddie smiled. "Yes, thanks."

Grabbing the light, he climbed the ladder and poked his head through the panel. Eddie's eyes searched for surveillance equipment. On the adjacent panel lay a dead mouse. He screamed as he fell back.

While Eddie erratically waved his arms, the swinging camping lamp struck the polystyrene ceiling panel and launched the mouse at Eddie's face. He screeched and jumped off the ladder. The mouse bounced off Eddie's forehead and landed on the grey carpet as Eddie fell on his side. His hands brushed every part of his body as if putting out an invisible fire.

Office workers stood in their cubicles to see what the commotion was. Rex noticed the mouse on the carpet and raised his hands to distract the workers from Eddie.

"Nothing to see here. It's a dead mouse," Rex said. "It's okay. We found a dead mouse."

Amongst the crowd, Bessie scrunched up her face in disgust.

Gary swished the last of his tea and swallowed. He narrowed his eyes. "You're a pest exterminator scared of a rodent?"

Eddie crawled back to his feet. "I thought it was something else."

Gary placed his hands on his hips. "Something ain't right about you two."

Eddie, aware all their eyes were on him, gulped. He never considered that he might actually find a pest, or be expected to respond as a professional on the subject.

"I'm not scared of a mouse," Eddie declared. "That would be unprofessional. We're professionals."

"Oh cool," Rex said.

Eddie turned around to see Rex on his knees. He held the mouse by its stiffened, straight tail.

Rex smiled. "It's like a lollipop."

Eddie gagged as he stepped back, bumping into Gary.

"Sorry," he said.

Gary grabbed Eddie by the collar, which caused the back of the jumpsuit to ride up into his buttocks again.

"You two are coming with me."

TWO

G ary shoved Rex and Eddie towards Dorian's office until Bessie stood in his way.

"What are you doing?"

"Ash has sent new spies," Gary said. "These two aren't pest control. They're scared of mice."

Rex held up the still dead mouse. "Do I look like someone scared of a mouse?"

Bessie rolled her eyes. "Unhand them."

"But they can't be trusted."

"Let them go."

Rex animated the mouse, turning to face Bessie and Gary as they spoke, as if it were listening to their conversation.

Bessie's brows snapped together. "Stop that."

Gary loosened his grip on the duo's collars. "Something ain't right."

Eddie raised his palms. "I tried to tell him I wasn't scared of the mouse, but he wouldn't believe me."

The large man leaned in. "Prove it."

"Come on, now." Eddie faked a smile. "How can I prove it?"

Rex stretched out his hand, offering the dead mouse to Eddie.

Gary nodded. "That works."

Eddie's jaw clenched as he leered at Rex. "Is that necessary?"

Bessie shrugged her shoulders. "Just do it."

He took a deep breath, reached for the mouse, and took it by the tail, his arm outstretched.

Gary folded his arms. "Hold it closer."

Eddie bent his elbow, bringing the mouse closer to his chest. He gazed off into the distance.

"Look at it," Gary said.

Eddie breathed deeply to avoid gagging. He made eye contact with the dead rodent. Rigor mortis had given the mouse a permanent, cockeyed stare.

After a few moments, Bessie cocked her head at Gary. "Satisfied?"

Gary nodded, turned around, and stomped off.

Eddie turned to thank Bessie, but she had already headed towards her desk. He dumped the mouse in the nearest bin.

Rex leaned over the bin. "I wasn't done with that."

Eddie lowered his voice to a whisper. "We don't have time to mess about. We need to be on the lookout for microphones or cameras."

"Do we have the bug detection device?"

"No, we can't afford the gear. I was hoping we'd spot something with our eyes. If we bought equipment, it would eat all our profits."

"What do we do if we don't find anything?"

"If it takes longer than a couple of days, we can buy the kit with our profits and sweep again."

"Okay, after we check the ceilings, do I get to check the air vents?"

"There's no air conditioning."

"But what about when Tom Cruise climbs inside air vents? I want to do that."

"That only happens in American movies. British buildings are older than plumbing, let alone air conditioners. Now get up there and look for bugs … The surveillance kind, not creepy crawlies."

Rex and Eddie spent the day climbing up and down the ladder as they worked their way towards Bessie's desk. From afar, she politely smiled at them.

"I'm getting a look from that Bessie," Rex said.

"What? No, you aren't. She's looking at me."

"Is not."

"Is too." Eddie spoke too loud.

Bessie scowled at the pair.

"Now you're getting looks," Rex said.

Eddie narrowed his eyes. "Will you please focus on the work."

Rex climbed up the ladder and lifted a ceiling panel. He smiled. "Hey, Eddie. Remember at school in year ten, when Mr Mundy said I would never be able to get an office job? Look at me now."

"You're dressed in a jumpsuit."

"Yeah, in an *office*. My nan always said I was clever enough to have an office job."

Eddie felt Bessie watching him, so he waved a device around to appear busy.

"What's that?" Rex said, on his way down the ladder. "You said we couldn't afford any bug detectors."

Eddie lowered his voice. "We can't. It's my dad's old pager." He opened his palm, revealing a cracked screen.

"Thought I could use it as a prop and pretend it's a bug detector."

"But we're pretending to be pest control."

"Not to her." Eddie nodded in Bessie's direction. "Dorian has to think he's getting his money's worth. And she's the one that's going to report to him."

Rex stood. "That's pretty sly, Eddie. I like it. Can I have a go?"

"No."

"I could use your phone."

Eddie waved the pager around, avoiding eye contact with Rex. "Use your own phone."

"Mine's well old. Everyone will know it's a giant phone."

"You're not using mine. You mess with the apps. Last time, I found a recording of you singing nineties TV theme tunes."

Rex pouted. "My one doesn't do recordings."

He grabbed a stapler from a nearby desk and swung it around while pretending to read a display.

From afar, Gary watched while taking a call. Rex gave a wide-smiled nod.

A nervous man in his early fifties dawdled past Rex and Eddie to the neighbouring desk. He had thin grey hair, a pale complexion, and gaunt cheeks. The man wore grey trousers, a white shirt, and a brown bow-tie. A few seconds after sitting down, the man jumped to his feet and scoured the office.

"Has anyone seen my stapler?" he called out.

None of the employees paid attention.

"Come on, who took my stapler. Everyone knows there are two designated staplers chained to the stationery cupboard. Mine is my own."

Rex subtly—or as subtly as Rex could—lowered the stapler out of view.

"This is unbelievable," the nervous man said. "I've tried being nice, I've tried leaving notes, I've tried hiding the stapler," the anxious energy in his voice faded as his bottom lip quivered, " but you all just help yourselves."

Rex and Eddie turned to each other with raised eyebrows.

The nervous man stepped out of his cubicle. "Do I have to come around and check every desk?"

The employees continued on their phones or keyboards while Gary stood, still on the phone.

The nervous man pointed at the detective duo. "You two? Have either of you seen anyone come by here?"

Eddie winced. "We, uh, we just look for bugs — I mean pests. Not that bugs aren't pests. Anyway, we didn't see who came past."

"You were right here, though. I'm not saying you saw them take my stapler, but who came by? Did you see anyone?"

Rex shook his head.

Eddie copied. "No."

The nervous man slumped into his chair and thumped his head on the desk. "My wife will leave my ears ringing if I tell her this happened again. She'll say, 'Francis, you let them walk over you every day.'"

Rex shrugged. "Don't tell her then."

Francis sat up and smiled. "I like that. That's not bad." He peered off into the distance. "Don't tell her…"

With the cubicle wall hiding Rex's hands from Francis's view, he tried to pass the stapler to Eddie, who batted Rex's hand back.

Rex side-stepped to a nearby bin and dropped the

stapler, he coughed as it hit the bottom to cover the sound. The pair moved their investigation closer to Bessie.

"Hi," Eddie said as he swept the sides of her desk with his pager.

Bessie rolled her chair to the end of the desk. She curled her top lip. "What's that?"

"It's a bug detector," Eddie whispered.

"How does it work?"

"Uh … Radio signals?"

"Doesn't that negate your pest control story?"

Eddie hid the pager under his palm. "I'll be more subtle." He waved his hand around her phone.

Eddie looked over to Rex, who stood a couple of cubicles away with Gary Allen. Rex smiled as he took a business card Gary handed him and approached Bessie's desk.

"I think we've got another exterminator job. Gary wants us to search his place for ants."

Eddie folded his arms. "More work as pest control?"

"Yeah, well, we got the costumes, right?"

"*Uniform*, it's called a uniform. And no, we aren't pest control."

"You said we needed clients that pay money."

"Guys," Bessie said. "You're on our time, so you should save your lovers' tiff for later."

"We're just business partners," Eddie said.

She nodded her head with mock-interest and glided her chair to her computer.

Rex and Eddie stood, unsure how to leave with any grace.

"Bessie," Rex said.

She didn't look away from the computer screen. "What?"

"Who do you think is the leak?"

Bessie sighed and rolled her chair towards them. "I don't know. I'm not sure there is one."

Eddie leaned in. "What do you mean?"

"Dorian gets a bit carried away with his imagination. He rewrites history a bit."

"In what way?"

"Ash Haynes was originally his business partner. They started this company together. That's why Ash knows the cleaning fluids formula."

"So Ash took the formula and started his own business?" Eddie said.

"They started the company after a night of cocktails with a business plan written on a napkin. I think Ash might just be following the business plan and Dorian thinks Ash is ripping him off."

Rex's jaw dropped. "They're both following the same plan?"

Bessie nodded. "Mostly. Ash pitched new ideas at the creative meetings, but Dorian always turned them down. Now, Ash has left, and Sparklefeet has stalled. Ash is doing what he wants, and his company is thriving."

"Where's the napkin?" Rex asked.

"Dorian keeps it locked in the safe in his office."

"Do you know the code?" Eddie asked.

Bessie shook her head.

Rex sighed. "We can't go back to Dorian and say he's the spy."

Eddie scratched the back of his neck. "Why has he hired us to find the leak if he's following Ash's original plan? He'll get caught."

"He must not realise it," Rex said.

Bessie grimaced. "When he told me to hire you, he said he wanted the cheapest detectives in town."

"We prefer 'most-competitive,'" Eddie said.

"I told Dorian the better-paid ones would be more successful, but he said no."

Eddie put his arms on his hips. "You think he's using us? Why?"

"Maybe he wants to muddy up Ash's name?" Rex asked. "Make him look bad?"

"Did he say anything else about hiring us?" Eddie asked.

"Not really." Bessie straightened her back. "Oh, he did get excited when I said you were the guys in the newspaper that accidentally stumbled on the Door Knock Killer last month. He laughed and said you were perfect."

"That was a successful investigation," Eddie said.

"Didn't you just walk in on your office maintenance man murdering someone?"

Eddie stuck his chin out. "Well … yeah, but it was a bit more complicated than that."

Rex folded his arms. "So Dorian hired us to start a rumour that Ash's company is ripping him off to make Dorian look more favourable?" He slumped into a nearby office chair. "We're on a wild goose chase."

Eddie stared at Dorian through his office's glass wall, shouting at the conference phone.

"A wild goose chase with billable hours," Eddie said.

Rex tightened his brow. "What's that mean?"

"We ride this out for every billable hour we can get, maybe we'll actually find the leak." Eddie turned to Bessie. "If it wasn't Dorian, who else could it be?"

THREE

After a few days of pretending to detect bugs and spying on the staff, Rex and Eddie had come no closer to their wild goose. Although Rex found the whole affair quite dull, Eddie relished the steady pay and offered to buy lunch.

The detective duo exited the office building and walked along the main road to a rustic café. The café was on the bottom floor of a stocky office building made of dark brown bricks, which had a fortress-like quality to it. A large window with 'Café de Paris' painted in cursive made the little restaurant quite inviting. Inside, the walls were sky-blue with farm knick-knacks on the wall. Country farm tables and chairs were placed in three rows across the café.

Rex and Eddie entered in their exterminator uniforms. The people in the queue gave them a wide berth.

Eddie curled his top lip. "Is it something we said?"

New customers walked in the door, saw the pair, and walked back out. Behind the counter, a brunette girl with thick eyeliner watched Rex and Eddie while taking orders.

"This place is nice," Rex said.

"We've earned it," Eddie said. "Two days billed and we've extended the contract. Order what you want, my treat."

"Cheers, Eddie." Rex smiled wide as his eyes scanned the blackboard menu behind the counter. "Ratatouille? Who'd want that?"

"It doesn't have a rat in it, it's a vegetable stew."

Rex frowned, unimpressed. "Like how mince pies don't have minced meat in them?"

"A bit like that, yeah."

"Le Truffle Burger. It says ground beef, but is that real or is that like ratatouille and mince pies?"

"It's real beef, it's a fancy burger with truffle oil."

"Hmm, I don't know about that. What's the difference between ground beef and minced beef?"

"Minced and ground are the same thing."

At the till, the brunette girl whispered to the manager, a plump man with wavy hair, a bulbous nose, and a thick, greying moustache. He sighed as he walked down the counter to Rex and Eddie.

"Hello, gentlemen."

"Hi," Rex said. "Can I get a chicken salad sandwich and—"

"I'm afraid I'm going to have to ask you to leave."

Eddie stuck out his jaw. "Why?"

The manager pointed behind them to a woman who spat out her sandwich and left.

"You're scaring away the customers."

Rex folded his arms "How's that our fault?"

"You're pest control. We are a kitchen, so people think we have a problem. You need to go."

"Come on," Eddie said. "People don't think we work here. We're in the queue."

The manager huffed. "Half the people have left since you entered, and no one's coming in anymore. This is our rush hour, we need the business."

Eddie huffed. "Fine. Come on, Rex. They just lost themselves, two customers."

"That's it, we're not ever eating here," Rex said. "We don't want your stupid, lame food anyway."

As they headed towards the exit, Rex picked up an abandoned sandwich with one bite in it from an empty table. "Except this one sandwich." At the next table, he grabbed a half-eaten brownie, "And this brownie." By the exit, he grabbed an open packet of crisps. "And then I'm never eating here again."

The manager chased them out of the door.

As they ran, Rex smiled. "At least we know the disguises work."

Rex and Eddie walked across the office building's car park on their way back to work.

"We should just park the car here," Rex said as he chewed on the claimed food.

"I'm not parking our old banger in front of the client. If they see that infernal machine, they'll question our professionalism. They'll start asking probing questions like, 'Do you have a detective licence?' and we don't want to disappoint them."

Rex tore his recycled sandwich and offered it to Eddie. "You need a detective licence?"

Eddie raised a palm to the food offering. "Not legally, but it looks good if you have one because they test your fitness and competence."

"We should get one."

Eddie let the awkward silence hang as they reached the entrance.

Rex swallowed the sandwich. "You can have a bite of the uneaten corner of the brownie."

Eddie held the door open. "No, but thanks all the same."

They took the elevator to the third floor and entered Sparklefeet's office. As they arrived, several members of staff had gathered around the open kitchen area.

"I'm sick and tired of it," a voice said.

The staff members stepped aside to reveal Francis Bard, the nervous man with the bow-tie, standing at the fridge with his arms crossed.

"Someone stole my lunch from the fridge." Francis slumped into a plastic chair by the kitchen table.

While everyone else ignored him, the pair approached Francis.

"Are you okay?" Eddie asked.

"No, I'm not."

Rex offered the open bag of crisps. "You can have the rest of my crisps."

"You'd do that?"

"Yeah."

"You'd give me a part of your lunch?" He lit up like he'd never seen such generosity. Francis took a bite. "Salt and pepper. Thanks so much."

"Don't worry about it," Rex said. "I didn't pay for them. They were left on a table at a café."

"Someone left an unopened bag of crisps?"

"No. It was opened."

Francis's chewing slowed. His mouth agape, the chewed-up sludge of the crisps sat between his bottom teeth. He swallowed and handed the bag back to Rex.

"You full?" Rex asked.

He nodded.

Rex finished off the crisps. "How long have your sandwiches been stolen?"

"A few weeks. This place has been going downhill for months now. Ever since Ash left."

Eddie raised his eyebrows. "You know Ash Haynes?"

"Oh, everyone knows Ash. He was the most popular guy here. Everyone wanted to work with him."

"You wanted to work at Klean Loafers?" Eddie said.

Rex leaned in. "Are you the double agent?"

Eddie slapped Rex's shoulder. "You can't ask that question, it's too rude."

"I wish I were a double agent," Francis said. "I mean, Ash is a great guy. I wanted to work for him, but he didn't take me."

Eddie pulled up a chair and sat. "So Klean Loafers poached Sparklefeet employees?"

"Ash took about a third of the company. All that's left is those he didn't want. Everyone invited joined him, he's a real leader. Sandwich thievery wouldn't happen under his watch."

"Any suspects?" Rex asked.

"I don't know. I wish I did. Some bastard, or a woman. It could equally be a woman in this day and age."

Eddie frowned. "I don't think women's equality paved the way for sandwich thieves, but I agree it could be a man or a woman."

Rex pulled Eddie aside and whispered. "We're already interviewing about the leaks. We can probably find the sandwich thief. Right, Eddie?"

"Dorian isn't paying us to find a sandwich thief. We have to stay focused on the case."

"But it's bad for morale, look how sad Francis is. If people can't trust the work kitchen with their lunch, what else can't they trust?" Rex turned to Francis. "We'll help you find the sandwich thief."

"You will? How?"

Eddie's jaw tightened as he stared at Rex. "We aren't here to find a sandwich. We're here to find the … uh, pests."

"We'll multitask," Rex said. "That's what office people do, right?"

Francis nodded.

Eddie pursed his lips. "Let's master uni-tasking first and work our way up, shall we?"

"Come on, Eddie. It won't hurt if we find the thief along the way?" Rex gave a needy smile which softened Eddie's resolve.

Realising he was being manipulated, Eddie turned away from Rex and accidentally locked eyes with Francis. For the first time since they'd met him, the man had a faint hint of hope on his pale face.

Eddie sighed. "Fine."

"Perfect, I'll sit with Francis and work out the details. Can I have the notepad?" Rex grabbed the notepad out of Eddie's hand and plopped in a seat with enthusiasm. "What kind of sandwich was it? I want to know bread type, fillings, any other distinguishing features? Square-cut or triangles, that sort of thing."

"Well, they're triangle-cut."

Rex nodded as he furiously made notes. "It tastes better triangle-cut."

Francis lowered his head.

"Eddie, can you get this man a tissue?"

A large hand reached over the detective's shoulders

and grabbed the notepad. The pair turned their heads to see Gary Allen standing behind them.

"What do we have here?" He flicked through the notes.

"Uh, that's private," Eddie said.

"Been keeping information on us, have you?"

Eddie raised his palms. "We can explain!"

Rex reached for the notepad, but Gary raised the book above his head. He pushed Rex over and searched through the notes.

"This what you're gonna tell Ash?"

"It's not like that."

"Everyone, everyone!" Gary called out. The office workers all paid attention from their various spots in the open office. "I've found the spies. These two right here."

Eddie stood, but Gary shoved him back down into his seat.

Gary's eyes burned through Eddie. "You think you can threaten my livelihood and get away with it?" He turned to Francis. "What did you tell them, you backstabbing little turd?"

Francis lowered into his seat. "My sandwiches were triangular."

Gary's forehead furrowed. "You what?"

Dorian marched across the office towards the kitchen.

"Dorian, I found the spies! I don't know how Ash did it, but he got these two to replace our pest exterminators."

"They're detectives, and you just blew their cover," Dorian said. "I hired them to catch the spy."

Eddie grimaced. "Spy isn't the right word."

Gary's eyes flashed at him. Eddie flinched.

"They'd be more of a double-agent," Rex said.

Eddie shook his head. "That's incorrect. It's simply an employee leaking information."

"A mole?" Francis asked.

Eddie winced. "That's not right, either."

"I don't care what they're called," Dorian shouted. "I care what they're doing." He huffed. "Gary, give them back their notepad. You two, go wait outside my office." He turned to the watching crowd. "The rest of you get back to work."

FOUR

Rex tapped his foot as the pair waited outside Dorian's office. Eddie checked his watch, not because he wanted to know the time, but because he felt awkward doing nothing. The office workers all observed the pair from their desks, whispering comments to each other.

The blinds over Dorian's glass walls slid open with a sharp screech. He waved them in. As he talked, his words were muffled by the glass.

Rex opened the door, and the two sat at Dorian's desk.

"What the hell is going on?" Dorian barked, his back facing them.

Rex and Eddie, wide-eyed, turned to each other.

"Uh…" Eddie began.

Dorian spun around to face them, revealing a Bluetooth device attached to his right ear. Pointing to the earpiece, he shushed them with a finger to the lips. Rex and Eddie nodded.

He sat down and stared them in the eyes. "You're

taking some liberties, I ought to come over there and beat you."

Rex straightened his neck. Eddie pointed to himself and mouthed, "Us?"

Dorian scrunched up his face and shook his head. The pair relaxed into their chairs.

"I'm gonna have to call you back," Dorian said. "And when I do, I expect some good news. You hear me?"

He clicked the Bluetooth earpiece, gave the pair a toothy smile, and leaned forward.

"What the hell is going on?" he shouted.

Rex and Eddie stared, unsure what to say.

"Us?" Eddie asked.

"Yes, you. Do you see anyone else in here?"

Eddie pointed at Dorian's earpiece. "No, but—"

"The two of you have been in here for three days, and I've not seen any progress. I thought I hired professionals."

"We've made progress," Rex said. "We found a mouse, a beetle, a daddy-longlegs. There's an ant problem in the kitchen you should get fixed."

"Ignore him," Eddie said. "We did a thorough search, and we found no bugs."

Rex raised his hand.

Eddie rolled his eyes. "No *surveillance* bugs."

Rex nodded as he lowered his hand.

"So, you've got no intelligence?" Dorian said.

"Eddie has a college degree," Rex offered. "I got two A-levels at school."

Eddie placed a hand on Rex's shoulder. "He means information."

Rex bit his bottom lip.

Eddie gave Dorian an apologetic smile. "We know there aren't any bugs, that's information."

"So how are my leaks happening?"

Eddie peered over Dorian's shoulder at the safe, wondering about the business plan napkin. Although he liked being paid, he hated to think Dorian was tricking him somehow.

"Well, that's the hard part," Eddie said. "Since there's no surveillance gear monitoring the place, that means the leak is human. An employee is feeding information to your competitor."

"A double-agent," Rex said.

Dorian stroked his chin. "A double-agent, huh?"

"Well, no," Eddie said. "I mean, it's not like they're an actual spy. It's a person sharing information with Klean Loafers, maybe forwarding a memo or an older document like a business plan."

"Sounds like a double-agent to me," Dorian said.

"But—"

Dorian pointed at the pair—it was quick and dramatic. "I don't care. You blew your cover. Give me one reason why I shouldn't fire you."

"Because…" Eddie's mind went blank.

"You'll never find out the spy if you fire us," Rex said.

"I'll just hire new undercover detectives."

"But everyone is suspicious now. No matter who you hire, everyone will know they're detectives."

Eddie nodded. "That's true. And we already know the staff. You'd have to start from scratch with new detectives."

Dorian relaxed into his chair. "I guess so."

Eddie smiled. "We can interview people and see who could have an allegiance to Ash Haynes and Klean Loafers. Do you have any suspicions?"

"None, that's why you're here."

Is that why I'm here? Eddie thought, staring at the safe behind Dorian.

Eddie bit his bottom lip. "What about the Monday

meeting attendees? I've heard that's where most new policy is first announced."

"You think the circle of trust has been broken?"

"It's the first place we should look. *Someone* in that meeting is the leak." Eddie widened his eyes to imply he meant Dorian.

Dorian sighed. "You can stay on. I'll email the staff to tell them they are to cooperate in whatever way they can."

Eddie raised a finger. "We'd need to book at least another two days on the job."

He nodded. "Fine. Now go find my spy."

The pair left Dorian's private room and travelled through the open office.

"What if there are bugs and we couldn't see them?" Rex asked.

Eddie put his finger to his lips. "Shush."

He pulled Rex into the men's room, a single-use toilet with a shower for the cyclist workers. Eddie locked the door and ran the sink. After staring at the shower, he turned that on for good measure.

Rex hunched up his shoulders. "What are we doing in here?"

"We don't know if bugs are listening or not, so we need white noise to talk privately. Now that we've got a few more days work, we can buy an actual bug detector from eBay. When it arrives in a few days, we'll do a real sweep. For now, we interview people." Eddie turned off the sink and shower. "Let's get changed, and come back fresh after lunch."

As the pair stepped out of the bathroom, a man waiting stared at them. He was tall and round with a goatee and shoulder-length hair. He folded his arms.

"You guys used the shower together?"

The detective duo gave a polite smile and kept on walking.

———

After lunch, the pair returned to the Sparklefeet office in their usual business attire. Eddie wore a polyester suit and tie, and Rex had put on his collared shirt, casual trousers, and corduroy blazer.

Rex smiled. "We should get back to Francis and gather intel on this sandwich thief."

Eddie rolled his eyes. "I'm going to do something relevant to the case. You've got five minutes. Then I expect you to join me."

"What are you going to do?"

"I'm gonna interview Bessie. Actually, make it ten minutes."

"Oh, I should join you for that."

"No, you get your sandwich intel. I'll interview Bessie, and we can meet up afterwards."

Eddie walked down the row of cubicles and rolled a chair to Bessie's desk. Her eyes narrowed slightly.

"Hi Bessie, I got a few questions regarding the leak."

She glared at him. "Fine."

He sat. "Dorian said new ideas are discussed at the Monday creative meetings. Since that's the first place a plan can leak, I'm planning to interview the attendees. I just want some background information. What was the last leak, the brushes thing?"

"Yes."

"And that was first mentioned at the circle of trust meeting?"

"I'll check the minutes." She opened up a document on

her computer and scanned through. "It was two Mondays ago."

"Does that document list everyone present?"

"Let's see. It was me and Dorian. Gary Allen."

"The sales guy?"

She nodded. "Francis Bard, who you just met."

"Yes."

"Kevin Grigsby."

"Who's he?"

"He's the IT guy. General support for computers, and he does our website. Have you met him? He has long hair and a goatee."

"Me and Rex met him on our way out of the bathroom."

"You were in the bathroom together? They're single occupancy."

"Well, we didn't know that until we went in, did we?"

"No need to be defensive." She scrolled the mouse. "Then we had our intern, Raymond Wilkins, so he can learn and make tea."

"How long has he been with the company?"

"Four months."

Eddie scribbled notes on his pad. "When did the leaks start?"

Bessie counted in her head. "About that time, but Ash only left two months before that. You think Raymond's the leak?"

"Ash left six months ago, then the intern comes in a couple of months later, and the leaks start. Why not him?"

She winced. "The others all worked with Ash, and they all loved him. Plus, Raymond is an idiot."

Eddie tapped his pen against his chin. "Might be an act. He pretends to be gormless, so no one suspects."

Bessie cocked her head. "I suppose that's your grand plan?"

Rex entered the cubicle with a wad of detailed notes in his hand. "What is a gorm?"

Eddie turned around and rolled his eyes. "Not now, Rex."

"He doesn't know," Bessie said.

"I do … I might … I know it's good to be gorm … or be a gorm … uh, to have gorm?"

Bessie typed on her keyboard, waited, and responded: "Gorm, less. Gorm from the Norse word for understanding, so not understanding."

Rex and Eddie cocked their heads.

"Wikipedia," she said.

"So you didn't know, either," Eddie said.

She looked him up and down. "I know it when I see it."

Bessie gave a mock smile, her white teeth shone in contrast to her ruby lipstick.

Raymond Wilkins, a slender nineteen-year-old with black, spiky hair and a crooked nose sat at his computer desk watching a series of parkour stunt videos. He wore bulky headphones that bled electronic music while he ate microwaved noodles. After each death-defying stunt played on his screen, Raymond would give a subtle nod of approval and say, "sweet" or "sick."

Rex and Eddie waved to get his attention, but he remained focused on the monitor.

The desk phone rang. Raymond took off his headphones and picked it up. "Yeah … Yeah … Yeah …

Nah … Okay." He hung up and went back to his headphones.

Eddie stepped to the neighbouring cubicle and picked up a phone. He dialled Raymond's number. Raymond removed his headphones and picked it up. "Yeah?"

"Eddie Miles, private detective standing to your right."

Raymond looked over and put down the phone. "Yeah?"

Rex offered his hand. "I'm Rex Milton—"

Eddie cleared his throat. "We're business partners."

Raymond breathed through his mouth, expressionless. "Yeah? What?"

"We're investigating the recent company leaks. Do you have any connections to Ash Haynes?"

"Nah."

"You attend the creative meetings on Mondays?"

"Yeah."

"What do you do during the meetings?"

"Make tea and coffee."

"And the rest of the workday?"

"Make tea and coffee."

The music blasting from Raymond's headphones interfered with Eddie's focus. "Can you stop the music for a minute?"

"Why?"

"It would be easier to focus on the task."

"I focus better with it."

Raymond shrugged and turned back to the screen. On the monitor, a hoodie-wearing man jumped and flipped over a pond. "Sweet."

"Nice," Rex said from the walkway.

Raymond turned to Rex. "Weren't it, though?"

"Definitely. Sick moves."

"Mate, you've got to see this one." Raymond re-wound

the video and showed a clip of a hooded man jumping across two pillars, up a wall, and into a window.

Rex offered a high five and Raymond obliged.

"So, you a detective then?" the intern asked.

"Yeah," Rex said with a smile.

Raymond bit into a protein bar and spoke with his mouthful. "Man, you've got to get this spy before he ruins this company, I was hoping to get a job out of this."

Eddie watched the two talk with disdain.

"We're trying," Rex said. "You notice anything suspicious?"

"I don't know, man. What're you looking for?"

"People acting weird."

"They're all weird, but that IT guy, he's sneaky."

Rex sat on the desk and whispered. "In what way?"

"People, right, they act like they're smarter than me, but they don't see what I see."

Eddie folded his arms. "What do *you* see that no one else can possibly see?"

"The printer. It's hidden behind the pillar so others don't notice, but where I sit, I see it all day. That IT guy, man, he's been printing out loads of stuff. He's always on the lookout, acting proper shady."

At the printer, Gary Allen grabbed papers from the document tray as he drank tea from a polystyrene cup. He stormed down the aisle past Rex, Eddie, and Raymond.

"Afternoon, fellas."

"Gary," Eddie called out. "Can we interview you this afternoon?"

"Can't, I'm heading to a golf game with a big retailer we're trying to get in bed with. You want to do a walk 'n' talk?"

Eddie marched along to catch up. "Come on, Rex.

Raymond, you see Kevin print anything else, you let me know."

Raymond curled his lip. "Who's Kevin?"

"The IT guy."

He half-nodded as he put on his headphones.

The detective duo followed Gary through a fire door into a stairwell. Black metal stairs made an echoing clunk with each step.

"I'm sorry about shoving you two about earlier. I get protective about the company, you know? Glad to have you on the same team."

"Yes," Eddie said, as they lightly jogged down the stairs.

"Guess I'll need to find another solution to my ant problem."

"Sorry about that," Rex said, chipper and enjoying the exercise. "Where are we going?"

"To the back car park, it's through the storage area."

"There's no lift?" Eddie asked.

"Lifts are for losers, you should always take the stairs. If you want to be in the elite, you need to work for it."

"By taking the stairs?" Eddie asked.

"It's what the stairs represent. You've got to hustle and climb to reach the top."

Eddie curled his lip. "But we're going down?"

At the bottom of the stairs, Gary opened a fire door and crossed through the lobby. Rex and Eddie followed him to a locked door. He swiped a keycard and entered a warehouse, two stories full, loaded with stacked pallets of Sparklefeet shoe cleaning products.

"You keep the product here?" Rex said.

"This is the storage section. You need a keycard to get in and out. Be careful what you put down here, or it'll get nicked. Raymond the intern put some kits together yesterday and said someone stole several washcloths while he wasn't looking."

"Another mystery," Rex said with a raised eyebrow.

Eddie rolled his eyes, which had begun to water. He sneezed. "Whatever's in that soap, I'm allergic to it."

Rex tutted. "Eddie's allergic to everything."

A forklift truck drove past them, carrying a pallet of shoe cleaner through the open port into the back of a van.

Gary passed through a door next to the port which led outside to the back car park. Rex and Eddie followed him down the concrete steps to the tarmac.

"That's my car," Gary said with a smile. He pointed to the red Jaguar taking two parking spaces. "Jag, 2008."

"Nice," Rex said.

Eddie, disgusted by Gary's car taking two spots, flared his nostrils, which set off another set of sneezes.

"One of the perks of having a keycard is when the front parking is full I can park back here. VIP." He unlocked the car with his key fob.

Eddie held the bridge of his nose. "Actually before you go, we're meant to be asking you questions."

Gary checked his watch, which twinkled in the sunshine. "Rolex," he said. "I've got time for one question."

Rex raised his hand. "Oh, me. Pick me."

Eddie put his hands on his hips. "That's not how this works."

"You." Gary pointed at Rex.

Rex smiled. "What tastes better, square or triangle sandwiches?"

Gary opened the car door. "Triangle. Always." He put on his sunglasses. "Ray-Bans," he said, and got inside. "Let me know if I can help with your investigation. I'm off to hustle."

The Jaguar's engine roared as the car drove to a tall, metal gate. The gate automatically slid open as the vehicle approached.

Eddie stomped through the warehouse to the lobby door with Rex close behind him. He attempted to open the door, but it was locked.

"No keycard," Rex said, sheepishly.

Eddie sighed. "Where's that forklift truck driver gone?"

"Dunno."

The loaded-up van drove from the port along the car park.

"Follow that van," Eddie said.

The pair ran out the warehouse as the van passed the gate. As they ran, the gate drew closed. Rex managed to squeeze through the gate just before it shut. He punched the air in victory. Exhausted by the stairs, Eddie felt a stitch in his gut which slowed him down. The gate closed.

Rex spun around as he cheered and calmed when he saw Eddie's stone-cold face between the gate's bars.

"You didn't make it?"

Eddie shook his head.

Rex poked his hands through the bars and crossed them. "I'll help lift you up."

"I'm not climbing the gate. There are spikes at the top."

"You can do it."

"This suit is new. Go get Bessie. She must have a key."

"Fine, I needed to ask her about the sandwich anyway."

FIVE

After Bessie let Eddie back into the lobby, Rex and Eddie returned to the Sparklefeet office. They walked over to the IT station, a cubicle in the far corner with the least amount of daylight. Kevin Grigsby, the overweight man from outside the bathroom, worked away at dual monitors, both displaying computer code.

"Are you Kevin?" Eddie asked.

He continued to furiously type. "Yeah. You're the two blokes that took a shower together?"

Eddie faked a laugh. "Ha, yes. Well, no."

Rex shook his head. "We didn't shower together."

"You entered, you showered, you came out together. I saw it."

"We were outside the shower the whole time," Eddie said.

"Why'd you turn the shower on then?"

"So we couldn't be heard, obviously." Rex nudged Eddie for validation.

"Sorry, guys. That's a little too much information."

Eddie huffed. "Not like that."

Kevin held a large fizzy drink and sipped from the straw. His other hand continued typing.

"We're detectives," Rex said. "We're looking for the mole."

"Not a mole," Eddie said. "That still has spy connotations."

"You want a spy?" Kevin said.

"Someone is leaking information to Klean Loafers. We've been hired to find them. Weren't you in the kitchen during lunch hour?"

"No, that's my busiest hour. With no IT calls, I can work on coding."

"No alibi, huh?" Rex said.

"No need, I'm not a spy."

"No one here is a spy," Eddie said. "It's the leak we want."

Kevin typed away. "I'm not the mole, either."

"Did you work closely with Ash?"

"Yeah, of course. Ash and Dorian were always a team, so I worked with both of them."

"What was the dynamic like?" Eddie asked.

"Ash was a hard taskmaster, but he was a just man, and looked out for people. He demanded a lot, and showed you could do more than you thought, like that cool teacher you respected."

Eddie took a seat. "Seems the work environment has changed a lot since he left?"

"Well, Dorian is a softie."

"He is?" Rex asked. "He shouted at us."

"Yeah, he doesn't like to be the bad guy, so he gets walked on a lot. I've been trying to gee him up. Get the blood flowing."

"Like a pep talk?" Eddie said.

"More like … re-writing his code. He's badly coded."

Kevin's eyes scanned the office floor. "They all are."

Eddie pursed his lips. "So Dorian shouted at us because you got him to?"

"You've been here three days and no results."

"He told you we were detectives from the beginning?"

"Yeah, he tells me everything during our morning coffee."

"You both have coffee every morning," Eddie said, "so you must be the first to know about everything."

"Yes, that's right."

Eddie rubbed his chin. "Ever seen inside his safe?"

"No, why? What's that got to do with anything?"

"Thanks for your time." Eddie turned and walked out of the cubicle.

"Just one more thing," Rex said. "Do you like triangle sandwiches?"

The next morning, Rex and Eddie drove the Morris Minor, their lime-green junk of a car. Eddie tapped the accelerator as they crept along a quiet road in the older part of Cloisterham. The town centre had free street parking, but carried the risk of leaving your vehicle next to crumbly brick walls, or wonky old Victorian buildings that leaned out towards the road.

Eddie hunted for a space to park in. He stopped to size up their car with the gap the street offered.

"Looks good to me," Rex said.

Eddie curled his lip at the car in front. "They could have moved a foot forward towards that driveway. I hate inconsiderate parkers."

"Maybe they were in a hurry."

"That's no excuse, I still wouldn't do it."

He struggled to parallel park into the small gap. As they got out of the vehicle, Eddie sighed at the sight of the crusty brick wall threatening to topple over the car.

"Maybe we should re-park?"

"We are a bit far from the client's office," Rex said.

"I mean that wall. You think it's gonna hold up?"

Rex smiled. "It's made it this far." He patted the wall with a series of hearty slaps.

"Cut it out," Eddie said as he jumped out of the wall's shade and into the middle of the empty street.

Rex smirked.

On their walk to the office, they passed the Café de Paris.

Eddie checked his watch. "We're a bit early, we could grab a sausage baguette?"

Rex smiled. "Yes, please. Are you sure they'll let us in?"

"We're in normal clothes, they won't even remember us."

"I could get the hat and glasses from the car boot?"

Eddie shook his head.

They entered the busy café and waited in line.

Rex examined the menu. "Maybe we could order a sandwich to go. We can use it as bait for the sandwich thief."

"No."

"We could expense it."

Eddie sighed. "You need to drop this sandwich thief thing until we know who's leaking information to Klean Loafers."

Rex shrugged. "Well, that's easy. Kevin did it."

Eddie turned to Rex. "Why is that so easy?"

"Dorian tells him all his secrets every morning, he doesn't like people, he doesn't hang out with people at lunch. He even said he likes Ash more."

"I don't think he said that. I mean, he respects Ash more."

"Yeah, and he's the least invested in the company. As the IT guy, he can read everyone's screen. He has all the information at his fingertips."

Eddie took a deep breath. "If he doesn't care about anyone else at the company and it's failing, he's got nothing to lose by helping Klean Loafers. Dorian sees him as helpful and trustworthy, so no one suspects him."

"That makes perfect sense," Rex said. "I bet he even steals Francis's sandwiches to misdirect everyone's attention."

"No, Rex."

"He probably doesn't even eat them, the psychopath."

Behind the counter, the brunette girl with thick eyeliner gave the person in front their change. Rex and Eddie approached the cashier till.

"Hi, we'd like two sausage baguettes, please."

From the kitchen door porthole, the manager watched. He stepped out and stood behind the girl.

"Not you two again," he said.

"What, we have the correct clothes on," Eddie said.

"Don't serve them," the manager said. "They cost me too much money, I lost half a day's profit because of you."

Eddie threw his hands in the air. "We were only here for five minutes."

"At lunchtime, then word got out we had a pest problem. I can't have you in here." The manager shooed the pair as he walked them towards the door.

Outside, Rex and Eddie stood confused.

"We can get a Tesco's meal deal?" Rex offered.

"Wait here." Eddie marched down the street and turned into the road where the Morris Minor was parked. A few minutes later, he returned in his pest control uniform, holding a clipboard with paper attached.

"Uh, Eddie?"

"One moment."

Eddie re-entered the café, stepped past the queue, and narrowed his eyes at the manager behind the counter.

"What is this?" the manager asked.

"As a loyal customer," Eddie proclaimed, so all could hear, "I wanted you to know immediately that the droppings we found and tested on your premises where that of a rat."

The manager's face turned red. Customers sitting down had either stopped chewing or were spitting out their food.

"We recommend immediate treatment of the whole restaurant. Rat poison, traps, etc."

The people in the queue stepped away from the counter and headed to the exit as a baffled Rex entered. Customers sitting down had all collected their belongings and left their tables.

"Of course, you'll need to close the kitchen for the foreseeable future, in the interest of public health and safety."

The manager ran out from the counter, his arms flapping, cheeks burning. He stomped into the kitchen and returned with a broom in his rattling hand.

Eddie swallowed. "Leg it."

The pair dashed to the back of the restaurant. Backed into a corner, they searched around. The only exit was by the counter, which the manager blocked.

Rex grabbed a chair to use as a shield. The manager passed Rex with his eyes on Eddie. Realising he was safe, Rex scampered towards the front door.

Eddie grabbed a chair and looked over at Rex in the

doorway. "Rex?"

The manager turned to him. "You can go."

Rex bobbed his head as an awkward apology to Eddie and walked out the door.

Eddie opened the drinks fridge and threw plastic bottles at the man. Most missed, but some were so shaken, their tops sprayed out high-pressure fizzy liquid.

As the manager swung the broom, Eddie pulled the fridge door wide open to block. The brush hit the door, shattering the glass.

Eddie dashed along the row of tables. Halfway between the manager and the front door, he had an escape route.

He ran but tripped on the chair Rex left behind. After clonking his head on the tile floor, Eddie shook himself to attention. The manager rampaged through the tables and chairs towards Eddie.

Rex leapt back into the café and grabbed Eddie by the arm. He pulled Eddie through the door and yanked him into the path of a short, brown-haired woman. The impact knocked off her sunglasses.

"Sorry," Eddie said. He picked the sunglasses up and handed them back.

Befuddled, she took them. "Thanks."

The manager jumped out the door, waving the broom. "You're banned for life!"

Rex and Eddie scrambled down the street.

As Rex overtook Eddie, he said, "Told you we should have worn a hat and glasses."

The pair sat in Dorian's office. Seated in his ergonomic chair, Dorian adjusted the Bluetooth earpiece and entwined his fingers.

"I'm not buying it," he said.

Rex and Eddie waited, unsure if he was on a call or not.

"You think it was Kevin Grigsby?" he asked.

Eddie bobbed his head. "We want to rule him out."

"I know Kevin, he's my confidant."

"Exactly," Rex said. "You tell him everything."

"Because I trust him. What are you suggesting?"

Eddie leaned forward. "I suggest you tell him you're changing the formula ingredients and then we'll see if he tells Ash Haynes. We believe he prints out the documents."

Rex handed over a thick stack of paper. Eddie tapped the pages. "If you give him this printout we made, then we can follow him to his drop-off."

Dorian flicked through the pages. "What is this?"

"Rex made it last night. It's a bunch of scientific information about soap he printed off the Internet. Just tell him you've worked out how to make your soap for half the price. That should get Ash Haynes's attention."

"But when Ash gets it, he'll work out it's nonsense."

"And by that time, we'll have proven Kevin is the leak."

Dorian agreed. When the pair left, he called Kevin into the office. From an empty cubicle, Rex and Eddie watched through Dorian's glass office walls. As Dorian handed over the paper document, Kevin nodded. He asked questions and took the copy when he left.

The pair watched Kevin work at his desk until five-thirty, shut down the computer, and put on his coat. He held up a worn-out, shoulder bag and checked inside. His hand brought out the paper document. With an assured nod, Kevin placed the paper back inside.

Rex and Eddie smiled and followed him out the office and along the river to the high street.

"This isn't the way to Klean Loafers," Eddie said. "They must have a meet-up arranged."

As the sun lowered, it turned the clouds a grey orange. Eddie buttoned his suit jacket as the temperature dropped.

Kevin crossed through the Cloisterham bus station towards the town hall, a three-storey stone-brick building with a copper-roofed clock tower. Rex and Eddie watched from a small green park. A marquee above the dark-brown arched doors advertised a Shakespeare play. As Kevin reached the box office, he checked to see he wasn't followed.

Eddie sneered. "A drop-off at an amateur theatre night? A bit elaborate, don't you think?"

"Corporate espionage is dangerous, Eddie. I bet he needs a public space to feel protected."

"What if he gets recognised?"

"You know who goes to amateur dramatics?" Rex asked. "The family of the cast. As long as none of the actors are related to his colleagues, it's fine."

Eddie shrugged. "I'll go along with it."

The pair ran for the entrance door. The marquee display proudly announced a live production of Macbeth.

A short woman in her sixties wearing a felt jacket and a large brooch raised her palm to stop them.

"Tickets are ten pounds each," she said.

Rex curled his lip. "For Shakespeare? Isn't he well old?"

"What's that got to do with it?" the ticket seller asked.

"There's a theatre on the high street showing movies that are six months old for two pounds each. You expect us to pay five times that for a play that's like, from a hundred years ago."

"It's over four hundred years old," she said.

Rex scoffed. "You're proving my point."

"We aren't actually here for the play," Eddie said. "A

friend of ours is here. He dropped his wallet, I just want to return it to him and leave."

The woman leaned on one hip. "It's ten pounds for entry. If you watch the show or not isn't of interest to me."

Eddie rolled his eyes and handed over the money. He turned to Rex. "We'll expense it."

Inside the crescent-roofed auditorium, the walls were painted royal red. The two hundred seats were a little worn out, and the stage was framed by a dulled brass proscenium arch. The pair studied the half-filled seats searching for Kevin.

"What does Ash look like?" Rex asked.

Eddie thought it over and slapped his forehead. "I don't know. I never thought to ask."

Rex and Eddie couldn't see Kevin amongst the sea of old people. As the lights dimmed, they took their seats.

"Crap," Eddie said. "We've blown our chance."

The curtain raised and the three witches played out the first scene. The lights faded to black. When the lights returned, men dressed as sixteenth-century soldiers stood on the stage. In the centre stood Kevin. He walked with buoyancy and declared his first line in a booming voice.

The pair watched in shock. This was Kevin's secret.

———

Rex and Eddie entered the foyer amongst the leaving audience.

"That was cool," Rex said. "All the violence and killings and stuff. I never thought of the past as being exciting."

Eddie searched for a backstage door. "We still don't know why he took the papers home. Come on. Let's talk to him."

As an usher exited a side door in the foyer, Rex and Eddie slipped through. Backstage they approached Kevin's dressing room and knocked. As he opened the door, his face dropped. He attempted to shut the door, but Rex and Eddie pushed it wide open.

Inside the dressing room, Eddie grabbed the record bag and pulled out the papers. He read the first page: '*Macbeth, a play by William Shakespeare.*' It was the playbook.

Kevin snatched the playbook back. "What do you think you're doing?"

"Investigating you," Eddie said.

"You think I'm the spy? I'm Dorian's confidant."

Eddie nodded. "Exactly, so you know all the inner planning."

Kevin's shoulders dropped. "That paper about the soap, that was a setup? Dorian doesn't trust me?" He slouched as he sat in his chair.

Rex patted Kevin on the shoulder. "It makes sense, you've got the most access. He talks to you. You can access the server and read all the documents and emails you want." Rex's eyes lit up, and he turned to Eddie. "He can access the server and read any document or email we want."

"Any document or email?" Eddie asked, turning to Kevin.

He nodded. "Any, but you can't tell anyone about my acting."

"Why?"

"It's just … I can't perform when I see people I know, but I can bare my soul to strangers."

"You were great," Rex said.

Eddie bobbed his head. "You give us access, and your secret is safe with us."

SIX

On Friday morning, Rex, Eddie, and Kevin arrived early at the Sparklefeet office. Kevin searched through everyone's emails with the detective duo over his shoulders.

By the time lunch approached, they had found nothing to imply one of the employees was the leak. In fact, most people used their email to share memes, cat videos, and gossip.

Kevin's software had the ability to view all the computer screens at once. His monitor showed a collage of various social media feeds, online videos, and puzzle games.

Eddie slumped back into his chair. "We were completely wrong about Kevin, and now we're completely clueless about everyone."

"There has to be a clue in there," Rex said. "We just need to weed out the non-clues. Find out who has a secret."

"The thing is, they all have a secret. Dorian keeps that

napkin in a safe, Gary manages to deflect all our questions, Kevin is a secret actor."

Kevin smirked. "All the world's a stage, and all the men and women merely players."

Eddie sat up. "We uncover stuff, but none of it is related. Something has to stand out, but what?" He stared out the window, hoping for inspiration. Outside, he saw Bessie pull up in a red BMW convertible. The new licence plate indicated her vehicle couldn't be more than six months old.

Rex stepped to the window. "How much does that car cost?"

"I don't know," Kevin said, his eyes still on the computer screen. "She got it a few months ago, brand new as well."

Eddie stood. "On a receptionist's wage?"

"I think she's a secretary," Rex added. "Do they get paid much?""

"Secretarial Assistant," Kevin said. "And no."

"So Bessie's making extra cash somehow?" Eddie asked.

"Yeah, but it can't be her," Rex said. "She's nice."

Eddie tilted his head. "She's not nice, she's pretty." He turned back to the window and watched Bessie walk to reception. "She has a new expensive car, that's suspicious behaviour."

Rex crossed his arms. "Surely, she's innocent."

"Do you have any proof?" Eddie asked.

"No, but you know what they say. You've gotta roll with the hunches."

Eddie shook his head.

The bug detection kit from eBay arrived at Eddie's flat on Friday afternoon. It was a small black box with LED lights and a retractable antenna.

On Saturday morning, Eddie picked up Rex and drove to the Sparklefeet office building. Eddie pulled up to the car park barrier and took a ticket.

"We're parking in the office car park?" Rex said, relieved.

"They're closed today. No one will notice the state of our vehicle."

The pair got out of the Morris Minor.

Eddie locked the driver door. "Since we've already charged Dorian for bug detecting, we need to do this sweep on the quiet."

They walked up to the entrance doors.

"Do we get paid overtime for this?" Rex said.

"No. It's a secret."

"Then how are we gonna get in?"

Eddie pushed the buzzer by the building's door. The tubby-faced security guard released the lock with a button at his desk. Eddie signed in with the security guard and walked into the elevator.

"He didn't ask us anything?" Rex said.

"Well, we've come here for three days straight, as far as the security guard knows, we're new employees. So we sign in like normal."

The lift door opened. The pair walked into the Sparklefeet office. Rex insisted on using the surveillance detector, so Eddie supervised him while he swept the office.

After a few hours of sweeping, they reached Dorian's office. Inside, Rex waved the detector around while Eddie searched through Dorian's drawers. The large, yet minimal desk contained nothing of substance. The top drawer was merely filled with plastic forks and napkins.

Rex knelt by the safe and pulled the handle.

"No such luck," Eddie said.

"I could call my mate, Jim Jams. He knows someone that can crack a safe."

From across the office came the sound of the main doors opening and closing. Eddie peeked through the glass wall and saw Dorian stride along the cubicles towards them.

"Crap," Eddie said. "Dorian's here."

He crawled under the large desk, pulling Rex down with him. They were hidden by the desk's side panels.

Dorian opened his office door, walked to his ergonomic chair, and sat down. Rex and Eddie held themselves in awkward poses to avoid knocking against their client's knees under the desk.

Dorian opened his laptop and typed away for several minutes. Eddie's neck and arms were already starting to feel aches in his contorted position.

There was a knock at the door, and Bessie entered. "The security guard just called to say Roger is on his way up. He just took the elevator."

"Have him wait a few minutes in the lobby, then call him in when I start shouting."

Under the table, Rex and Eddie gave each other confused looks.

"Yes, boss," Bessie said.

"Who shall I be shouting at today," Dorian asked.

Bessie chuckled. "You want to pull that same trick on your uncle?"

"Of course, this is a negotiation. I need to start from a place of dominance."

"Why not the two numbskulls?"

"Oh, yes. They'll do."

Bessie closed the door. Dorian continued to type. After

a few minutes, Dorian cleared his throat and put on his Bluetooth earpiece.

"What am I paying you for?" he shouted. "You've been here for several days, and I've seen no results, aren't detectives meant to detect? Isn't that in the title of your job?"

Eddie's jaw dropped in shock. Rex pointed at himself and mouthed, "Us?"

"Then, tell me what you've found … That's not good enough."

Bessie re-entered. From under the table, Rex and Eddie saw a set of legs in suit trousers and Oxford shoes.

"I expect results!" Dorian shouted. "I expect you in my office first thing Monday with evidence, you hear me?" Dorian hung up the phone. "Hi, Roger. Take a seat."

Roger sat down and stretched his legs out under the table. Rex and Eddie shuffled into a smaller space to avoid contact.

"It displeases me to talk of such ugliness," Roger said in a velvety-soft, posh voice. "But I'm afraid I have no choice."

"This quarter has been challenging," Dorian said.

"When I invested in your company, I intended to remain a silent partner. My motive was merely to give you the capital you need, and you've wasted it. It's my belief you've lost control of your company, and I need to hire a new CEO."

"Please, Roger. I know we're facing some tough challenges, but I have a solution."

"Yes, I heard. Those local boys playing detective. Such antics make you look foolish."

Annoyed and defensive, Eddie straightened his neck, bumping his head under the table.

"What the devil was that?" Roger said.

Rex and Eddie skulked under the table, panicked.

A second knock came from the door. Bessie entered. "I've got two coffees."

She stepped to the desk, placed them down, and left.

"I have a solution that I think you'll be happy with," Dorian said.

Rolling the chair back a foot, he spun around and typed his pin code into the safe. After the safe beeped, Dorian opened the door, revealing a stack of cash on top of a pile of papers. He picked up the money and placed it on the table.

"One hundred grand," Dorian said.

"You want to buy me out?"

"It's your original investment, your shares are currently worth a little over ninety-six. You can keep the change."

"They were worth three times that six months ago, before your clumsiness."

"And I'm sorry they aren't now, but Klean Loafers is trouncing us. Things are so risky, I don't want you to suffer if it doesn't work out."

Roger grumbled. "I assume you've already drawn up the papers."

"I have."

Dorian returned to the safe and took out the contract, revealing the signed napkin underneath.

"Let me put on my glasses," Roger said.

The sound of the wall clock felt deafening in the silence.

Rex's eyes pointed to the napkin in the open safe.

Eddie shook his head.

Leaning out from under Dorian's desk, Rex reached under their client's chair and over the wheels. Eddie reminded himself to breathe as he watched his partner sneak towards the safe. Rex extended his arm, but his fingers were a little too short of the napkin. He placed his free hand on Eddie's shoulder, who protested by rapidly shaking his head. Ignoring him, Rex used Eddie as support, leaned forward, and pinched the napkin between two fingers.

Eddie's arms buckled under the weight. Rex's hand pushed Eddie towards Roger's knee, so he had to try hard to stay central as Rex slithered back between Dorian's chair and the desk.

Rex had almost made it all the way back under the desk when Dorian tucked in his chair, running over Rex's supporting hand.

Rex's mouth opened wide, but he didn't make any noise. He placed his injured hand in his armpit. Eddie's eyes bulged, shooting Rex a deathly stare that clearly said, "Don't make a sound."

Dorian stared down at his feet.

"Are you okay, Dorian?"

Dorian's chair shuffled around. "Yes, thought the carpet was uneven, but it looks fine."

As Dorian stood, Rex and Eddie turned pale.

From under the desk, they heard the sound of a cup hitting wood. Roger backed away from the desk as a cascade of coffee poured off the table landed on Eddie's backside. Burnt, he leapt forward, head-butting Rex. Rex lost his grip of the napkin contract which slid out to the side of the desk.

"I'm sorry, Roger," Dorian said.

"Another clumsy mistake."

Dorian opened his desk drawer. A few napkins glided down to the floor, covering the napkin contract.

Roger leaned down and grabbed all of the napkins.

Rex and Eddie both flinched, wanting to snatch it back but stuck hidden under the table.

The table above them pattered as the two men wiped up the spilt coffee. A clump of heavy wet napkins dropped into the wastepaper basket next to the desk.

Rex and Eddie's shoulders sank.

"I think it's best I take that money off you before you pour my coffee on it," Roger barked.

He signed the contract with a furious scribble, stood, collected his money, and proceeded out the door.

Dorian sat back down and sighed. A few seconds later, Bessie returned.

"How did it, go?"

"I'm now the full owner of Sparklefeet."

"Congratulations. Anything else for today?"

"That's it. Enjoy the rest of your weekend."

Dorian placed the signed contract in the safe and closed it. Once Bessie and Dorian left the office, Rex and Eddie crawled to the wastepaper basket. They attempted to find the napkin with Dorian's business plan, but the paper towels were now one brown mush with blue ink streaks.

Rex and Eddie continued to search the entire office for surveillance devices, sweeping each cubicle as they passed. Eddie signed into a computer as Rex waved the detector about.

"You okay, Eddie?"

"I think Dorian is using us."

"In what way?"

He pointed at the monitor. "This is Sparklefeet's stock, the prices dropped after he hired us."

"They've been dropping for months."

"I know, but I can't help but feel we're being played. Did he use us to get his uncle to sell? Or was he honestly trying to do right by his uncle?"

"He seemed pleased," Rex nodded. "Maybe he believes in us and knows we're gonna find the mole."

"'The two numbskulls'?"

"To be fair, Bessie said that, not Dorian."

Eddie folded his arms. "He didn't argue."

They approached Bessie's desk where Rex waved the detector.

"Nothing. Did the batteries run out?" He threw his arms up in defeat and the LED lights flashed.

"It's found something," Eddie said.

Rex lowered the device to see, but the flashing stopped.

"Point it at the ceiling again."

He raised the device until the LED light flashed.

"A flash," Rex said. "Now what?"

Both detectives climbed the desk. The LED light flashed faster. Eddie gazed up at a tiny hole in the polystyrene ceiling panel, a black dot.

He pulled the panel down. "What do we have here?"

A small camera was taped to the back of the panel. Eddie pulled it from the panel.

"Someone installed a camera?"

Rex's jaw dropped. "So Bessie is being watched."

"Yeah."

Rex smiled. "Which means she's not the mole. The mole spied on her for secrets."

Eddie examined the bug. "It doesn't have a microphone."

"So the mole reads her computer screen?"

Eddie raised the panel and checked the hole's trajectory. The camera pointed down to her chair.

He shook his head. "I think it's looking down her top."

"The mole's a pervert?" Rex asked.

Eddie scratched the back of his head. "I don't think the pervert and the leak are the same person. We need some technological assistance."

Rex's back straightened. "Let's go see Kevin."

SEVEN

At Cloisterham Town Hall, Rex knocked on Kevin's dressing room door. Kevin opened the door while tying an embroidered cape around his neck. He rolled his eyes at the sight of Rex and Eddie.

"I told you I can't help," he said.

Rex barged in. "We'll only be a minute."

Eddie offered the surveillance camera to Kevin. "Please, help us."

"It's the weekend, I've got a matinee in twenty minutes."

"Fine," Eddie said. He raised his hand clutching a spread of Macbeth flyers. "I'll just put these up around the office on Monday. I was thinking the notice board, the bathrooms, and every desk."

Kevin gritted his teeth. "Okay, okay." He snatched the surveillance camera and sat at his dressing table. After rolling up his ruffled sleeves, he studied the camera.

Rex and Eddie leaned over his shoulders.

"Sorry, about the blackmail," Eddie said. "We need the camera back before the peeping tom realises it's gone."

"This is my time to prepare for the performance." Kevin studied the camera. "There's no memory card slot, so it must stream the video feed online."

"Over wi-fi?"

"It would have to be. There's no phone reception in the building. Dorian says it's because of all the layers of lead paint."

Rex pointed at the camera. "If it's wi-fi then it must be a Sparklefeet employee who knows the password."

Eddie nodded. "Can we connect to the feed and rewind to see who installed it?"

"I'm afraid not. The most you can do is reset it. Insert a pin into the device's reset hole, and it will do a factory restore. Then you can set up your own feed with your own password."

Eddie thought about it. "What good is that?"

Kevin straightened his jewellery band in the mirror. "When the owner finds out his feed is broken, he'll go check the camera. If he does that you'll have footage of him tampering with the bug."

"That's genius," Rex said.

Eddie scratched his cheek. "Unless there's footage of us taking it down, can't they look at that?"

"Not if the batteries died, which it looks like they did. Little camera like this would need charging every couple of days."

"Right," Eddie said. "So the peeping tom will need to collect the camera to charge it?"

"Exactly. I'll get it sorted for you on Monday."

Eddie's mouth twisted to one side. "We've got to get this set up before the owner finds out. Every second, we risk losing our lead."

"Guys, I perform in eighteen minutes. I've got to be

mentally prepared. I'll do it first thing Monday morning, I swear."

"Okay," Eddie said. He turned to Rex. "Would you care to join me for a bit of theatre?"

Rex put on an exaggerated smile. "Why, yes indeed. I'd love to see a play."

Kevin's eyes shifted between the pair. "You can't be in the audience, I'll freeze up."

"We were there last night," Eddie said.

"But now I know about it, you'll ruin my performance."

"We're big fans." Rex gave a thumbs up.

Eddie nodded. "In fact, I think we're free to go to every show between now and Monday morning."

Kevin reluctantly pulled a laptop from his shoulder bag and opened it on the dressing table. He charged the camera with a spare USB cable. While he typed, he occasionally brushed the massive costume sleeves up his arms. Kevin turned the laptop screen to Rex and Eddie. On the monitor, a webpage showed the camera's feed, a fisheye view up Rex's nostrils.

Eddie snatched the camera from Rex. "That's unnecessary."

Kevin sat back. "You know, by reinstalling this, you could get in trouble for spying on Bessie."

Eddie curled his lip. "But we didn't install it."

"The first time," Kevin said.

Eddie's jaw tightened. "What else can we do?"

"It doesn't seem connected to the case, maybe walk away before you get in trouble."

Rex smiled. "Or we could rescue Bessie from a predatory digital lurker, and become her hero."

Kevin pushed the laptop to one side and re-applied his

make-up in front of the mirror. "I thought her fancy car means she's the mole?"

Eddie huffed. "That's true."

"Is she going to think you're the hero when you get her fired?"

"But if we save her from the pervert," Rex said, "she might forgive us when we dob her in."

Kevin powdered his face. "And then you'll live happily ever after?"

Rex nodded. "Probably. Why not?"

Kevin turned around to face them both. "Which one of you will she live happily ever after with?"

Rex and Eddie both eyeballed each other.

The door knocked, and the stage manager opened the door. "Kev, you're on in five."

Kevin stood. "The course of true love never did run smooth."

On Monday, Rex and Eddie arrived at the office and spent the morning staking out Bessie's desk. They hoped to catch the peeping tom checking his camera or find evidence that Bessie was the mole.

Although they hung back a few cubicles, Bessie knew they were watching and gave them dirty looks. Eventually, she became so annoyed with the constant whispers and peeping over the wall dividers that she jerked her head at them.

"What are you two playing at?" Bessie asked.

"Nothing," Eddie said

"Nothing," Rex repeated.

"You're investigating me, aren't you?"

Rex nodded. "Yeah."

Eddie shook his head "No."

"We are, though," Rex said.

Eddie raised his palms. "Only in the sense that everyone is a suspect. So, please go about your business like normal."

"Yeah, 'cause if you stop, we can't catch you."

"Rex, shut up." Eddie turned back to Bessie. "Everyone is a suspect, that's standard procedure."

"You haven't ruled out anyone?" Bessie asked. "After a week of working on the case. That sounds incompetent to me."

Eddie's jaw went slack. "I mean … we ruled out some people, but that doesn't mean we won't put them back on the list."

Bessie sighed. "You can investigate me if you want to waste your time. I'm the most dependable person I know. I wouldn't tell anyone anything about Dorian."

"Well, you just told us that. That's something," Rex said like he caught her in a trap.

Bessie scrunched up her face and returned to the computer. Eddie peered up at the tiny hole in the ceiling. It seemed off.

He whispered to Rex. "Is that different to you?"

Rex bit his lip before returning to a confident smile. "Nah. It's your imagination."

Eddie narrowed his eyes. "What have you done?"

"Nothing. I didn't do anything."

Eddie marched over to an open computer in a nearby cubicle. He typed in the video feed's web address and watched footage of the kitchen fridge.

Rex leaned over Eddie's shoulder. "That's odd."

Eddie rewound through hours of people going in and out of the fridge. "You relocated the camera to the fridge."

"It wasn't me."

The feed showed sped-up backwards footage of Rex placing the camera in the kitchen. Eventually, the footage returned to Bessie at her computer with her low-cut top on display.

Passing by, Francis peeked over the cubicle's wall divider and saw the webcam feed of Bessie. "What's that?"

"Nothing," Eddie said.

He tapped random keys to turn it off, but accidentally pressed a zoom button which cut to a close-up of her cleavage.

Francis stepped back "You can get arrested for this sort of thing."

Eddie waved his hands. "It's not what it looks like."

Rex clicked refresh, and the feed returned to a live feed of the fridge. "I fixed it. See, we're gonna catch your sandwich thief."

Francis watched the feed and turned to Bessie at her desk.

"But you spied on Bessie. I should report that."

"No, no." Eddie gently pulled Francis into the cubicle and lowered his voice. "We found the camera set up to spy on Bessie, we want to capture the person that installed it."

"To impress her," Rex added.

Francis's nervous eye-shifting calmed. "You think she'll be impressed if you find out someone is spying on her?"

Rex nodded. "Yeah, why?"

Francis pointed at the pair. "Bessie, these two weirdos have been spying on you."

Rex gawked. "Francis, you idiot, don't you want your sandwiches?"

Bessie marched over. "What's going on?"

Eddie closed the web browser window. "Nothing."

Francis folded his arms. "They had video of you, spy camera footage."

"He's a liar," Eddie said.

Bessie pulled Francis aside. "Francis, you have to stop this."

Francis lowered his voice to a gentle whisper. "I'm trying to look out for you."

She turned her face away. "I've already told you. I'm not interested."

Francis peered down at his shoes. "Then, can I have the car back?"

Bessie stared at him as she folded her arms. "You said that was a gift."

"It was, but—"

"But when you bought the car, you thought you could buy me?"

As Bessie stormed back to her seat, Francis scratched the back of his head, defeated.

Rex and Eddie had been standing awkwardly close. When Francis saw them, his eyes welled up. Rex gave a gentle wave. Francis fled to the fire door and entered the stairwell.

Rex cocked his head. "What's happening?"

Eddie folded his arms. "Bessie isn't the leak."

The pair followed Francis up to the roof of the building. He stood at the corner wall and gazed over Cloisterham's modest skyline, a few grey office towers built in the seventies next to an octagon-shaped shopping centre. The little metropolis was surrounded by ancient forts, war memorials, and Victorian buildings. Following the River Invicta, the sun shone over Cloisterham Cathedral and the Norman Castle.

Eddie slowly approached. "Francis?"

"This is none of your business." He clutched the safety rail by the roof's edge.

Eddie struggled to find the appropriate words. "You all

right … mate?" He winced. Eddie always felt like a fraud saying 'mate'.

Francis took a deep breath and stared down at the street below. "You ever get vertigo?"

The two detectives reached the edge and peeked down. Eddie felt a little dizzy. Rex seemed to have no idea of the potential danger. They both shook their heads.

"I do. I look down there, and I feel that urge to jump. I'm sure it feels like flying … until the end."

Rex and Eddie gave each other a worried look.

"That's not vertigo," Eddie said.

Francis glared at them. "It's not? What is it then?"

"I don't know. A death wish? Suicidal tendencies?"

"Oh." Francis sat on the concrete ground, huddled up in a little ball.

Eddie joined him. "You bought Bessie that car, didn't you?"

"What of it?"

"And now you're broke?"

"I messed up." Francis's voice cracked. "It was our savings. I have shares in Sparklefeet, but they're worthless now. My wife doesn't know how bad our finances are, so I thought I could fill our savings back up by cutting a few corners."

"Like packed lunches?" Rex asked.

"Don't be silly," Eddie said. "You can't get a car's worth of savings with a few years of packed lunch, right?"

Francis's face turned white.

"That's your plan?" Eddie said.

"I was hoping to get a raise or two as well."

"When do you retire? Five, ten years?"

Francis sighed. "I've messed up, boys. I thought I could depend on this job, but the company is going under."

Eddie sat on the concrete a few feet from Francis. "You're the leak?"

Francis's head jolted up. "I'm not, I'm not a spy. I swear."

"You have the biggest motive," Rex said.

Eddie nodded in agreement. "Your wife finds out you bought a young woman a new car, I'm betting you'll get divorced."

Francis forced a laugh. "My motive is to save the company. When this job ends, I'm stuck. No job, no savings, no wife."

"Definitely no Bessie," Rex added.

"Thanks for reminding me."

"You can't take the car back?" Eddie asked.

"I put the title in her name. It's all hers."

Eddie sighed. "If you help us find the leak, we could secure your job."

Francis buried his head in his hands. "Providing Dorian doesn't find out the head of finance is broke. I'm so embarrassed."

Eddie shuffled closer to Francis. "There, there. We all feel like that sometimes. Everyone's a pretender, really."

"Yeah?" Francis looked up, with a hint of a smile. "What about you two? You're successful detectives."

Eddie lowered his voice. "This is our first paying case."

Francis laughed through his nose. "Really?"

"Yep."

"We're not even licensed detectives," Rex added.

"Ha! You mean I haven't got professionals looking for my sandwiches?"

Eddie nodded. "We only created a detective agency because if we were our own bosses, we couldn't get fired."

Rex grinned. "And the thrills."

Eddie bobbed his head. "We both have different reasons."

"We still have a professional attitude," Rex said. "We'll find the sandwich thief, right Eddie?"

"If it's still a secret that the camera is there," Eddie added.

The sound of a woman clearing her throat broke their conversation. All three turned to the fire exit.

Bessie stood in the doorway with her arms folded. "Dorian wants to speak to you two, now."

EIGHT

Dorian stood over his desk and adjusted his Bluetooth earpiece. Rex and Eddie shuffled in their seats with nervous discomfort.

"I've seen some shysters in my time, but you disgust me." Dorian sat down, his steel-blue eyes seethed at Rex and Eddie. "I'm gonna make sure you never work again, you hear me?"

Eddie raised a finger, "I think that's a bit harsh—"

Dorian raised his palm. "Don't come crying to me when it doesn't pan out, because we are through."

He bashed his fist on his desk, his eyes still on Rex and Eddie. They sunk further into their seats—neither felt brave enough to call him out on the fake phone call.

"What are you jokers up to?" Dorian rotated his laptop to reveal footage of the kitchen fridge. "Do you take responsibility for this?"

Eddie winced. "Well…"

Rex gave a sheepish nod.

"I hire you to find a spy and instead, you're caught setting up spy cameras. Do you work for Ash?"

"No. Not at all," Eddie said. "Did Bessie find the feed?"

Dorian folded his arms. "*You* will do the talking."

Eddie wriggled in his chair. "Okay, we found a camera."

"So Klean Loafers does have a spy?"

"It seems unrelated. Someone was filming Bessie, and we found the camera, so we know she's being spied on. But I think it's unrelated to Ash Haynes. It's some pervert watching Bessie, but we haven't found out who the pervert is yet."

"I'm not paying you for that. Why's it in the kitchen?"

Rex perked up. "To find the sandwich thief."

"I'm not paying you for *that*, either."

"You should," Rex said. "Morale is low because people can't even trust their colleagues with their lunch."

Dorian leaned his palms on the desk. "I don't care about the sandwich. I want the mole found. You got it?"

"Got it," Eddie said. "We've both got it, right Rex?"

Rex shrugged to suggest he wasn't entirely onboard.

"He's got it," Eddie added. "Don't worry about him."

Dorian sat back in his chair. "Bessie said she overheard you tell Francis you aren't licensed detectives?"

"Is Batman a licensed detective?" Rex asked. "No, and he's one of the best ones."

"If you don't solve this case this week, I'm not paying you."

Eddie curled his lip. "Uh … what if we don't want to solve the case, and we just leave now?"

"Then you won't get paid for the days you've already done."

"Harsh," Rex said. "Harsh, but fair."

Eddie folded his arms. "How is it fair?"

Rex shrugged. "I don't know. I hear people say that sometimes."

Dorian pointed to the door. "Get out, find the mole."

Eddie stood. "How did you know about the fridge video?"

"You're being broadcast online. A friend of mine noticed the Sparklefeet Industries heading on the kitchen's notice board and sent me a link."

"Who's broadcasting the feed?" Rex asked.

Eddie got closer to the laptop. "Everything is in Japanese, but it looks like it's a site for watching women. What kind of a friend sent this?"

"More of an acquaintance, really. He said your video stream got more popular now it's filming people opening and closing the fridge."

"How did you know we did it?"

"I used a translating website, with mixed results, but the comments talk about two idiots installing the camera above a girl's desk—"

"We just put it back," Eddie said. "To find the owner."

Dorian raised a suspicious eyebrow. "The comments also mention one of the idiots moving it, that's when the stream went viral."

Rex grinned. "Wow, we're big in Japan!"

"Not for much longer, you are to go in the kitchen and take it down. Also, what's this about you both using the single occupancy bathroom together? The whole office is talking about it."

As Dorian spoke, the feed showed someone go into the fridge and pull out Francis's lunch.

"The sandwich thief! We can catch him red-handed. " Rex said.

"I don't care about the thief."

Eddie leaned in. "It's happening. Whose hoodie is

that?" Eddie said. "Their face is in shadow. It could be anyone."

Rex stood. "We have to go to the kitchen, now."

Dorian pursed his lips. "Are you listening to me?"

"Dorian's right," Eddie said. "It's not the case."

Rex backed away towards the door.

"Rex, sit."

"I'll be really quick. I just need to know."

Dorian's eyes narrowed. "Don't you walk out of here while I'm talking to you."

Rex exited.

Eddie stood and raised his finger. "I'll get him back here. I promise."

———

Rex dashed along the row of cubicles towards the kitchen area.

Eddie stumbled after him. "Rex, you're gonna get us fired."

The sandwich thief saw them coming and stormed out of the kitchen.

"Hey!" Rex shouted.

Before either detective could get a good view, the thief pulled up their hood and ran towards the fire exit behind Eddie.

Eddie raised his hands. "Okay, calm down. We're just—"

The thief shoved past Eddie, knocking him to the ground as he opened the fire exit and escaped into the stairwell.

Rex helped him up. "You okay, Eddie?"

Eddie narrowed his eyes as the door closed. "Let's get him."

The detectives ran into the stairwell. Eddie looked up while Rex checked the lower flights of steps from the bannister. Below them, a door automatically closed, creating a metallic thunk.

"He's one floor down, " Rex said.

They barrelled down the flight of stairs. The door led them into the second-floor lobby as both of the lift doors closed.

Above the elevator doors, a display indicated one elevator went down while the other travelled up.

Eddie stomped his foot. "He could be in either one. We've lost him."

"The security cameras," Rex said. "I'll go down and see if I can find him."

Rex hurried down two flights of stairs. He burst through the fire door, panicking the security guard. The tubby man's feet darted off the desk as Rex run at him with breathless enthusiasm.

Rex examined the monitors, three rows stacked on each other, showing black and white videos of each floor at various angles.

"There." Rex pointed at the monitor showing the hooded thief in the fifth-floor lobby.

Rex searched the desk and grabbed the intercom system's gooseneck microphone. He pushed the red button and broadcast to the whole building.

"Eddie, he's getting off the lift on the fifth floor."

On the screen, the thief gave the security camera the finger.

"Rude," Rex said.

"You can't use the intercom," the security guard said.

Rex tightened his grip on the microphone. "I'm commandeering this desk for my investigation."

"Under whose authority?" The guard asked.

"Under the same authority as Batman—justice!"

One row down, they watched Eddie bolt up the stairs to the fifth floor.

"Eddie, he can hear me. You'll have to be faster."

The thief ran through the double doors of another company's office.

The security guard curled his lip. "What's going on?"

"He's a thief. We have to catch him."

The guard narrowed his eyes, distrustful of Rex.

"Dorian West demanded it," Rex said.

The security guard straightened his hat and sat up in his chair. Both men watched the monitors with eagle eyes.

"Where're the cameras for actual offices?" Rex asked.

The security guard lowered his head. "We don't have any."

"What?"

"We've got a few dummy cams in the offices, but I only monitor the open areas."

On screen, Eddie reached the fifth-floor lobby, holding his side like he had a stitch.

Rex pushed the intercom button. "He went into the office."

Eddie nodded at the camera.

"I can't see in there, though. We've got no cameras in the actual offices."

Eddie glared at the camera and raised a finger to his lips.

"Oh right, can't say anything that helps him," Rex said.

Rex winked at the monitor displaying Eddie. The watching security guard tucked his chin in and scrunched his brow.

Frustrated, Rex placed his clenched fist on his lips, waiting for inspiration. On a pillar next to the desk, he saw a laminated floor plan highlighting fire exits. The eager detective ripped it off the wall and slammed it on the counter.

He pointed to the office area. "Where are the exits?"

The security guard checked over the plan. "Just the lobby and the outer stairwell."

Rex gestured at the bank of monitors. "Where's the outer stairwell?"

The guard pointed at an empty stairwell on screen. "That one."

Rex searched through the other stairwell screens. All he saw was someone casually walk down the stairs. He glanced through the other cameras but saw nothing of note. The thief would still be in the office.

Rex stared at the desk phone. "What's an extension number for the fifth-floor office?"

"Depends, who do you want to call?"

He shrugged. "Anyone?"

The guard opened his folder and called out, "Five-six-four-three."

Rex punched the numbers into the phone.

"Hello?" a female voice said.

"I'd like to speak to Eddie Miles, please."

"No one named Eddie Miles works here."

Rex bit his bottom lip. "He'd be the madman running through the office."

"Which one?" she asked.

"Uh, the slower one?"

Eddie ran through the fifth-floor office. It was the exact layout of the Sparklefeet office. He slowed to a stop as unfamiliar staff members stared at him.

He shook off the false feeling of déjà vu and searched each cubicle for the thief. A woman screeched as he poked his head over the wall divider.

"Excuse me, sorry."

As he hunted for the thief, sweat beads trickled down his face. He was hot. He considered taking off his new suit jacket, but didn't want people to see his sweaty armpit patches.

After searching four workstations, he browsed the entire floor.

"Has anyone seen someone in a hoodie run through here?"

No one bothered to answer.

"Probably holding a sandwich?" Eddie added.

Two rows away, a middle-aged woman with cat-eye glasses stood from her desk.

"Eddie Miles?" she called out.

"Yes?"

"I've got a call for you."

Eddie spun around and leapt into the cubicle of the same screeching woman. She screamed again as Eddie grabbed her office phone from over her shoulder.

"Sorry, again. What's your office extension?"

She placed her hand on her heart. "Five-two-two-one."

He raised the phone and called out to the woman in cat-eye glasses.

"Forward it to five-two-two-one," he shouted

The phone rang in Eddie's hand.

He lifted the receiver. "Hello? Rex?"

"I've lost him, Eddie. He has to be in that office with you. There're only two ways out, the lobby or the outer stairwell, and I haven't seen him on the security cameras."

Eddie looked back at the lobby entrance and forward to the stairwell fire door.

"What's your number?" Eddie asked.

"What's our number?" Rex said, his voice turned away from the phone.

"One thousand," the muffled voice of the security guard said.

"I heard," Eddie said. "Keep an eye on the cameras. Don't say anything over the loudspeaker that will help him."

Eddie hung up and speed-walked towards the stairwell door, checking each cubicle as he passed. As he neared the end of the row, he paused. In the corner of his eye, he noticed the tip of a green sleeve hanging over the lip of a rubbish bin.

He pulled the sleeve from the bin revealing a green hoodie. The thief had changed his outfit.

Eddie grabbed a cubicle phone and dialled one thousand.

Rex picked up the phone. "Eddie?"

"He's taken off his hoodie, he's wearing something else, and possibly acting calm. Can you recheck the outer stairs?"

Rex studied the various stairwell feeds on the security monitors. One floor showed a smoker by an open window. A second floor showed someone pacing as they spoke on a phone. The third screen showed someone walking downstairs.

"A smoker, someone taking a call, and a..." Rex watched the screen closely. No facial features could be made out, but he noticed the person's jaw move. "He's chewing! He's eating the evidence!"

"Where?"

"Stairwell, second floor."

"I'll call you back."

Rex watched the screens as Eddie burst into the stairwell. The metal flooring must have made a thunking noise because on the monitor below, the chewer looked up, alert.

Eddie took off his shoes.

"What's he doing?" the security guard asked, enthralled by the escapade.

"Socks, the silencer of the foot," Rex said with a broad smile.

Eddie bolted down the stairs and off-screen. Below, the chewing thief shrugged off the noise and continued at a leisurely pace. As Eddie ran, Rex and the guard watched him leave one screen and appear on the next. He was one floor away from catching the thief, but his socks slid, and he fell on his back.

Alerted by the noise, the chewing thief looked up the stairwell as they passed the person on the phone. The caller finished his call and returned to their office through the fire door.

Swallowing his food, the thief held his phone to his head and covered his face by scratching the back of his head. Eddie hurried down the stairs and ran past the thief.

The security guard drew a sharp breath like he was watching a sport.

Rex grabbed the intercom and shouted at the microphone, "You passed him, he's on the phone."

On the monitor, the chewer gave the camera the finger.

"That is rude," the security guard said with a tut.

The thief dashed through the fire door.

Rex pushed the intercom again. "He's run into the office now, Eddie. Sorry."

Eddie stomped back up the stairs and through the fire

door.

Rex and the security guard watched the second-floor lobby monitor, waiting for the thief and Eddie to run in. The security guard, enthralled by the chase, ate a crisp and offered the packet to Rex. Without taking his eyes off the camera, Rex grabbed a handful of crisps and shovelled them into his mouth.

On camera, the thief entered the lobby. He slowed as if struggling to run and digest his stolen lunch at the same time.

An unsuspecting Gary Allen exited an elevator around the corner and walked towards the office entrance with a cup of tea.

Eddie exited the office and nearly grabbed the thief until Gary stepped out from the corner. The thief bumped into Gary, knocking over the tea. Hot drink sprayed everywhere. Eddie backed away to avoid a scalding, but tripped on a door stopper and fell back.

Gary threw his arms in the air as the thief reached the lifts and pushed the call button. Impatient, the thief pried the elevator doors open. Rex and the guard watched in anticipation. The monitor feed fizzed and wobbled before turning to black.

The security guard sighed. "Not now." He bashed the top of the monitor twice, but nothing happened.

"Come off it!" Rex shouted.

The guard gave the monitor a sharp, loud whack and the feed returned.

Eddie got back on his feet and turned the corner. The elevator doors were closed, and there was no sign of the thief. He noticed a phone on the wall and dialled one thousand.

Rex watched Eddie call the phone and picked it up before the first ring could even finish.

"Hello," a posh lady said. "There are people running around the building and—"

"Not now!" Rex hung up.

The security guard flinched. "You'll get me in trouble."

"Sorry."

The phone rang again. Rex snatched it.

"Did you put me on hold?" Eddie asked.

"No, the line was busy."

"Busy!" Eddie shouted. "I'm busy."

"I know, sorry. It was bad timing."

"Where is he?"

Rex sighed, as he checked the lobby stairwell feeds. They were all empty.

"You're not gonna like it."

"Where is he?"

"He pulled the lift doors open, and we lost the feed. I think he climbed inside the lift shaft."

Eddie turned to the elevator doors. "Sod that."

"But he'll get away with it!"

Eddie hung up the phone and slowly approached the elevator door. He pulled the doors apart and peered inside. The lift lowered down, passing the floor with the silhouetted figure of the thief standing on top of it.

Rex and the guard watched in anticipation, wondering what Eddie would do.

The phone rang again.

"Excuse me, but I was just very rudely hung up upon by—"

"Hold, please," Rex said in a pleasant tone and hung up.

The security guard bobbed his head. "Better."

Rex leaned over the security guard's desk to the ground floor's foyer and checked the elevator display numbers. The thief's elevator approached the ground floor.

"Push the button for down," he told the security guard. "It'll stop it going to the basement."

The security guard, who looked like he had not exercised in a decade, tottered across the foyer. His feet were tiny compared to the rest of his round frame. He pushed the call button with his small hands, every other part of him had ballooned from years of sitting on the job.

Rex watched Eddie run down the stairs towards the basement. He grabbed the intercom to tell Eddie but realised he didn't want to give away the plan to the thief. How could he tell Eddie to come to the ground floor?

Ground beef is minced beef, he thought.

He pushed the intercom button. "Minced beef?"

On the monitor, Eddie stopped halfway down a staircase and listened to the announcement. He ran back up to the lobby.

Rex jumped. "Yes!"

Eddie shoved the fire door open as he entered the ground-floor lobby.

With a ping, the elevator doors opened. The security guard stepped inside and held the hold button.

"He's trapped up there," the security guard said, his face rosy from the adventure.

Eddie pulled open the second elevator doors. From above, legs kicked out and knocked Eddie to the ground. The thief landed in the foyer and ran for the front entrance.

"Parkour?" Eddie said as he nursed his hurt chin.

Rex rode out of the security guard desk on the rolling chair. He jumped from his seat and tackled the thief. The culprit wiggled and wormed across the tiled floor, but Rex straightened on top of him.

The security guard tottered over and held out a can of pepper spray. "Calm down, or I will spray you."

The thief surrendered to his capture. As Eddie caught up, they turned the thief around. It was Raymond the intern. He had red on his fingertips and across his shirt.

"Are you bleeding?" Eddie asked.

"Nah," Raymond said.

Rex pulled the flattened sandwich remains from Raymond's shirt pocket. "It's beetroot. I told Francis to make a sandwich with beetroot in it because it stains everything."

"Caught red-handed," the security guard said, impressed.

Rex nodded with a grin. "Exactly."

"Why'd you do it?" Eddie said.

"I don't get paid, I gotta eat, ain't I."

"Why Francis?"

"He's the finance guy, he can afford it."

"The man's in debt, he's a wreck, and you've pushed him over the edge."

Rex and Eddie pinned Raymond's arms and took him back to the Sparklefeet office.

As they entered the office, Eddie put on a serious expression, while Rex smiled.

"We got him," Rex said. "Here he is, ladies and gentleman."

The staff rose from their cubicles to watch.

"Raymond's the spy?" Gary Allen asked as he poured himself a fresh cup of tea.

Rex shook his head. "No, the sandwich thief."

The staff rolled their eyes and sat down.

As they passed the kitchen, Rex and Eddie took a bow to the secret fridge camera and pointed at Raymond.

Dorian stood outside his door with his hands on his hips. "You two. My office. Now."

NINE

Rex and Eddie sat across from Dorian's desk. Raymond stood at Dorian's side while Kevin propped himself on the side table. Eddie showed the video playback of Raymond stealing the sandwich.

"The security guard witnessed it all," Rex said. "He'll testify."

"The camera footage is clear enough," Kevin said.

Dorian turned to Raymond. "You stole Francis's lunch?"

"Yeah."

Dorian sighed. "Go put the kettle on and make everyone a cup of tea."

Raymond walked towards the office door.

"Is that it?" Rex asked.

"Raymond," Dorian called out. "Make sure you say sorry to Francis."

Raymond nodded and headed out the door.

Eddie glared. "What's happening?"

"Yeah, we solved the case."

Dorian cocked his head. "You found the mole?"

Eddie sunk in his seat.

Rex's voice lowered. "Well, no. Not that case."

"That is the case." Dorian raised his hands in the air. "There is no other case."

Eddie gave Rex a scornful glare, tipping the blame at him.

"This was important work," Rex said. "His actions slowly destroyed the office's morale, he literally ate away at their productivity."

"I've had the landlord complain that my staff have gone wild, running around other tenants' offices." Dorian narrowed his eyes. "I'm assuming you moving the camera means you'll never catch the peeping tom now."

Rex and Eddie both looked down at their shoes.

"Probably not," Kevin said standing from the side table. "They lost the peeping tom's original feed. He's not gonna come for the camera now everyone knows about it."

Dorian leaned forward. "What do you say to that?"

Eddie's heartbeat quickened. This was his one chance to prove himself as a professional and he blew it, unless he could find some way of fixing everything now, maybe with a speech, even a sentence would do. He turned to Rex, who politely smiled.

We're finished, he thought.

Rex drew in a deep, long breath that got everyone's attention.

This was it, Eddie thought, *maybe Rex had an answer.*

Rex sighed out all his air. Eddie waited for a conclusion, a response, anything. His last hint of hope died.

"Who put the feed online?" Rex asked.

"What?" Dorian said.

"Kevin reset the camera to factory settings. We put in a new password. So how come it still streamed to the pervy website?"

Eddie sat up. "Rex is right. The camera connected to the site, so the owner must have reconnected it at some point. Show us the webpage."

Dorian typed in the web address and spun the laptop to face them.

Eddie noticed the user profile name, Bard77. He clicked on it. The profile page had no personal details.

"Francis Bard?" Rex said. "Of course, it was him!"

"It's Kevin," Eddie said.

Kevin folded his arms. "How dare you."

"That's a serious accusation," Dorian said. "What do you have to back up your claim?"

"Bard. The bard. Shakespeare. Kevin loves Shakespeare."

"I do not," Kevin said. "The two shower mates would know more about Shakespeare than the IT guy."

"Seriously, Kevin," Eddie said. "You want us to drag Dorian to the town hall theatre tonight?"

"He acts in the plays," Rex said.

Kevin pursed his lips. "Et tu, Brute?"

Rex shook his head as if he felt a shiver. "My hearing went weird."

Eddie pulled a folded booklet from his pocket. "I've still got the playbill. He's an amateur actor in a local Shakespeare company."

"He's well good, too," Rex added.

Dorian glanced through the booklet. "Fine, so he likes Shakespeare. According to the website, 'the bard' is used by at least seventy-six other people."

Rex pointed at Kevin. "What year were you born?"

"I don't see what that has to do with anything," Kevin protested.

Dorian crinkled his nose as if a bad smell wafted in. "Seventy-seven. We're the same age."

Rex and Eddie jumped from their seats.

"We did it!" Rex raised a celebratory fist in the air.

"He never factory-reset the bug," Eddie said. "Kevin faked it so we'd put it back. All he had to do was never collect the camera, and we'd give up."

Rex opened his arms to offer a hug. Eddie grabbed one of Rex's hands and turned the embrace into an awkward handshake.

"If you didn't move the camera to the fridge, then we'd have never got caught, and neither would Kevin."

Rex smiled. "I did this?"

"Yes. Your unprofessionalism solved the case."

Dorian turned to Kevin. "You spied on Bessie?"

He slumped onto the side table. "I did it. I'm sorry."

Dorian sighed through his nostrils. "You're fired."

Raymond returned with four cups of tea on a tray.

Rex pointed at him. "What about Raymond?"

"He's my nephew."

"Ah," Rex and Eddie both said.

"He's staying, or my sister will kill me. Plus, it's not like I'm paying him."

Eddie curled his lip. "But you'll fire Kevin?"

"What he did to Bessie is sexual harassment."

Rex smiled. "So we did a good thing?"

Dorian shook his head. "You put the camera back up. Which means you either aided a sexual predator, or you *are* sexual predators. The three of you belong on a list."

"Yeah?" Rex asked, thinking it was a good thing.

"You don't want to be on a list," Eddie assured him.

"Oh." His smiled turned into a frown.

"Now get out. You're fired as well."

Rex threw his hands up. "What? Why? He found the sandwich thief, we found the pervert. We just need a little more time to find the mole."

Eddie put a hand on Rex's shoulder. "Leave it, Rex."

"But we're on a roll. You give us the rest of the week, and I'll bet we find who's stealing the cloths from the warehouse as well."

Dorian put both hands on the table and leaned forward. "You. Are. Fired."

Raymond grinned as he placed the teas on the desk.

"Fine," Eddie said. "But I'm invoicing you for the work we did."

"I won't pay it."

"Then I will come back here and—"

"You want money from me, you'll have to sue. In court, I'll make it known you set up a camera to spy on my assistant, and you physically assaulted my nephew. Do I make myself clear?"

Rex and Eddie walked out of the office with their heads low. As they passed Francis's desk, he gave them an appreciative nod, small enough that the others wouldn't notice.

At the elevator lobby, Raymond replaced the water cooler bottle and stared at the pair. They stepped inside the lift. Rex and Eddie both gave him the finger as the elevator door closed.

"Eddie, does that mean we're broke again?"

"Yep. We can try and sell the bug detector on eBay. That at least means we'll have some cash."

"Maybe Francis will pay us for finding the sandwich thief?"

"He might make us lunch, but that's about it." Eddie sighed. "I really wanted to know who the mole was."

"Me too, I'll always wonder. Like that time I saw an iguana at the bank. I should have asked people, there and then, what it was doing there."

"You saw an iguana at a bank?"

"Yeah, years ago. I lose sleep wondering about it."

Eddie shrugged. "Well, we've been fired."

"I thought being our own bosses meant we couldn't be fired. Why don't we solve it anyway?"

"How?"

Rex shrugged. "We could ask Ash Haynes who he hired?"

"Go to Klean Loafers? Are you joking?"

"What's the worst that could happen? He says no?"

Eddie's neck straightened. "You're right, only we can fire us. Let's solve the case."

The Klean Loafers office was a converted warehouse with red brick walls and high ceilings. Minimal furnishings, desks, and communal spaces were scattered around the polished concrete floor.

The receptionist took Rex and Eddie's names and directed them to a set of white, large, low sofas with overly stuffed cushions. Rex dove right in. While Eddie lowered himself down, the slow sink into the cushion had an unnerving, quicksand effect.

A tanned, confident man with wavy, black hair paraded towards the reception. He smiled at each worker as he walked. Each employee smiled back.

Noticing the man was headed towards them, Eddie patted

Rex's shoulder. Both attempted to stand but struggled, as if the giant sofas had their own gravitational pull. Rex rolled out to the floor and offered his hand to Eddie. Eddie grabbed the hand and skidded along the concrete floor as he got to his feet.

Ash stood close, but far enough away to show disapproval. "You two about to break out into dance?"

Eddie snatched his hand from Rex's grip. "Ash Haynes?"

He nodded. "Milton and Miles, right?" He offered a handshake with a smile.

"Yes, Eddie Miles. And this is my business partner, Rex."

The pair walked with him through the office. All the desks, chairs, and shelves were white. Every area was decorated with potted desert plants.

Ash guided them to a conference room with four glass walls. The tables and chairs were white. A line of air plants hung above the table. All three sat down.

"So, you find spies?" Ash asked.

"Yeah," Rex said.

"Well, we … uh … leak is the correct—" Eddie went quiet as Ash's smile faded. "Yes, we find spies."

Ash leaned back in his chair. "How can I help?"

"Dorian West believes you have a spy at Sparklefeet leaking information to you."

Rex cocked his head. "Tell us who the spy is?"

Ash half-shrugged. "If I knew, I'd tell you."

"You don't know who your own spy is?" Eddie asked.

Rex raised his eyebrows. "That's *deep* undercover."

Eddie sighed. "So, there is no spy. It's the napkin all along?"

Ash frowned. "What?"

"Bessie said Dorian and you wrote down a business

plan on a napkin. The reason both companies are copying each other is because they both use the same plan."

Ash rolled his eyes. "Did you see the napkin?"

Eddie bobbed his head. "No."

"Yeah," Rex said.

"Well, kind of," Eddie added.

Ash rested his arms on his desk. "It's not a business plan, it's a contract that we were gonna be best friends forever. Dorian kept it?"

"Yes," Eddie said. "But it was several sentences long, it said more than that."

"We were drunk, we said we'd always be best friends, go on holiday together every year, and make sure our future children were best friends, too. I think we set a spending limit on all Christmas and birthday gifts as well. We were very drunk."

"We should make a contract like that," Rex said.

"Not now," Eddie muttered. "Why do you think he'd keep it?"

Ash intertwined his fingers. "It also said we'd be fifty-fifty owners in all new businesses. Sparklefeet is dying. I think Dorian is orchestrating this whole thing so he can create the idea that I'm ripping him off. He'll then use the contract to sue for co-ownership of Klean Loafers, on the basis that I caused him to lose his own business."

"What if," Eddie said, "you paid us to destroy that napkin?"

"No good, it's notarised, he can get a copy from the notary."

Eddie grimaced. "You got a napkin notarised?"

"We were very drunk."

Rex snapped his fingers. "If he wants a stake in your company, maybe that's why he bought out Roger. Now

Roger won't have a claim to Dorian's share of Klean Loafers."

"It's an interesting story," Eddie said. "But maybe you're messing with us so we don't find your spy."

Ash leaned forward. "I'm telling you, I didn't hire anyone. All I know is we implement a new strategy, and then Sparklefeet launches it at the same time."

"This is confusing," Rex said.

Eddie tucked his chin in. "You don't know who proposes your business's strategies?"

"I work on the bigger picture. I have a team that works together. If one of them is getting leaked information, it's not at my request."

Ash invited them to look through his digital contact list and profiled each member of the team. As they studied the information, they found a similar name.

"Barbara Allen," Eddie said. "Is she related to Gary Allen?"

"Divorced," Ash said. "They parted before I left Sparklefeet."

"What does she look like?"

Ash clicked her profile, and her employee ID photo came up. She was a short woman with brown hair and thick forehead creases between her eyebrows.

Rex snapped his fingers at the monitor. "That's the woman Eddie bumped into outside the café. She dropped her sunglasses when we busted the place for rats."

"The woman you threw me at," Eddie said. "I bet she was in the area to meet Gary."

Ash stroked his chin. "Barbara, really? I had the creative team vote for their team leader, she won and got a pay raise."

"So she's been pitching stolen ideas in the meeting?" Eddie said.

"She's been doing so well, I was considering making her an executive, but I can't have her ruining my reputation." He huffed in frustration. "I'd fire her if I could prove it."

Eddie sat forward. "Let us get proof."

Ash cocked his head. "How?"

Rex curled his lip. "Yeah, how?"

"We fake information," Eddie said. "We give Gary a real scoop that forces them to meet. If Kevin can still access the company email, we'll get him to message Gary as Dorian. All we need is a, uh … a one thousand pound retainer?"

"You want me to hire you to find a spy in my own company? Why would I do that?"

"Because…" Rex said, stalling. "Because … if we stop the leak, we can save Sparklefeet, your reputation, and Dorian won't get shares in your company."

Eddie sat up. "That's right. If we prove she and Gary are ripping off Sparklefeet, you fire her, and Dorian can no longer blame you."

Ash thought it over. "Deal. But Dorian can't find out I'm involved. He won't believe me. You'll have to take the evidence to him."

The next morning, the pair parked the Morris Minor outside the Sparklefeet office. They watched and waited until Gary exited the building on foot. Rex and Eddie got out of the car and scuttled across the road to catch up with him.

"This is it, Rex. They can't escape us now. We get close, we record the conversation, and solve the case."

Gary opened the royal blue door of a brown brick building and entered.

Rex followed him, but Eddie froze.

"What's up, Eddie?"

Rex turned back to the door as he realised that Gary Allen had entered the Café de Paris.

"Ah," Rex said.

Eddie curled his top lip. "Ah, indeed."

TEN

E ddie paced the street outside the Café de Paris while Gary made his order inside. He noticed Barbara Allen walking towards them. Rex and Eddie snuck behind a bus stop shelter and watched her enter the café. As she waited in line at the counter, the manager walked amongst three rows of tables, delivering food to customers.

Through the windows, Eddie studied Gary Allen as he took his cup of tea from the counter. He shuffled down the aisle and sat down at a table in the back of the restaurant. Gary shifted in his seat, pouring sugar in his tea.

"It's over." Eddie banged his head on the bus stop pole in frustration. He held his forehead, surprised by the level of pain. "The one meeting that solves our case is happening in the one place we can't go. Now what?"

A huge grin grew on Rex's face. "Hats and glasses! I kept them in the car boot and everything. We'll wear a disguise."

Before Eddie could protest, Rex sprinted back to the Morris Minor while Eddie watched Barbara advance in the queue. Rex returned wearing a trilby hat and reflective aviators. He handed Eddie a pair of John Lennon-style sunglasses and a grey baseball cap.

"Excuse me," Rex said in a deep voice. "Do these belong to you?"

Eddie saw his own disdainful expression reflected in Rex's glasses. "You're serious?"

Rex smiled and raised the sunglasses. "It's okay, Eddie. It's me."

Eddie snatched the items from Rex's hands. "Yes, I know it's you."

"Oh, because you were expecting me."

"No, because you're just wearing a hat and glasses."

Rex helped Eddie put on his disguise. "You look great."

Eddie checked his reflection in the bus stop's glass. "Your trilby is a little attention-seeking, don't you think? We'll probably get noticed by Gary and Barbara."

Rex shrugged. "I can't think of what else we can do."

Eddie straightened the baseball hat. "Fine. I'll go in and record their conversation on my phone. I'm the least conspicuous. Your job is to go up to the counter and get served."

Rex pouted.

"If the manager catches you, make sure he's so busy kicking you out, he doesn't notice I'm there. Can you do that?"

He thought about it. "Yeah, I can."

Rex and Eddie entered the café and paused. The staff at the counter continued to serve the customers.

So far, so good, Eddie thought.

He nudged Rex, and they took a few steps into the café. Eddie walked down the closest aisle to the window. As he walked towards Gary Allen, he noticed the manager clearing a table ahead.

Oh crap, he thought.

Before the manager looked up, Eddie turned around a hundred and eighty degrees. The other aisle to Gary Allen's table was blocked by a young mother's buggy. There was no way to get past. He checked down his aisle, and the manager looked straight at him.

Eddie spun around and marched to the counter. He shuffled to Rex's side.

"Don't turn around. I've been rumbled," Eddie whispered. "We're swapping places."

He slid the smartphone across the counter to Rex. Eddie studied the round security mirror in the top corner, which gave a view of the whole restaurant. In the mirror, he could see the manager approach the counter with purpose.

"Now," Eddie muttered. "Go, I'll distract the manager."

Rex grabbed the phone. He walked along the aisle, passing the manager with his head down.

Eddie waited at the counter for the manager, who came right up next to him.

"What do you think you're doing?" the manager asked.

Eddie hesitated, his eyes focused on the menu.

"You need to offer a receipt. We always offer a receipt."

"Sorry," the waitress said back. "Won't happen again." She turned to Eddie. "What can I get for you?"

The manager brushed past Eddie and passed through the kitchen doors. Eddie turned to Gary's corner as Rex sat down at the neighbouring table, pretending to read the phone.

"Sir?" the waitress asked.

Eddie faced the waitress with his mouth agape. In a moment of panic, he'd handed over the investigation to Rex. Now, every second was a moment of panic.

"Are you ready to order, sir?"

"Um, coffee?" Eddie didn't drink coffee and was surprised by his own request.

"What kind?"

"A medium one?"

"Latte? Americano? Cappuccino?"

"A normal one. Whatever the normal one is. A black coffee ... with milk? Is that a thing?"

Barbara joined Gary at the table as Eddie paid for his drink.

"It'll be right up," the waitress said.

Eddie pretended to check the drinks fridge as an excuse to get closer to Rex and the Allens.

Barbara added sugar to her coffee.

"You back on the sugar?" Gary asked.

"Yeah, what of it? You're the one who has too much tea."

Gary raised his cup. "Not anymore. This is my first cup in a week."

Rex looked up sharply, offended by the lie. The Allens shifted along their table after his head sprung up. Luckily for Rex and Eddie, no one wants to look at a weirdo. Instead, they kept the strange person in their peripheral vision and looked around him.

"Regular coffee with milk," the waitress yelled out.

Eddie bit his lip as he stared at the Allen's table.

"Hey, baseball hat!" the waitress shouted. "Coffee with milk is done."

Eddie snapped out of his gaze and walked back to the counter. After grabbing the cup, he edged past the fridges towards Gary and Barbara to make sure he could hear them.

Rex pressed the record button on the phone's audio app.

Barbara stirred her drink. "So what have you got for me this time?"

"I think we should stop this arrangement. Sparklefeet has suffered enough. Any more leaks are going to completely destroy the company. I quit."

"Fine. I'll take my alimony instead."

"Okay, I can do that. The full month's worth."

"And the back alimony."

"You want six months of alimony?" Gary asked. "That's not the deal. I gave you information instead."

"Unfortunately, our unofficial agreement won't be counted by anyone else." She dropped the pleasant tone. "I'm legally entitled to all six months."

The manager passed Eddie with a tray of food and placed a turkey sandwich in front of Gary.

Rex leaned too far forward, and his trilby fell off his head. He tried to grab it as it fell to the table, but instead he launched the hat at the manager's feet.

The manager picked it up. He stared at Rex and paused.

"Sorry," Rex said in a hoarse tone to cover his voice.

"No, it was my fault," the manager said and handed him the hat.

Rex smiled.

Gary and Barbara leaned in closer, lowering their voices to a whisper.

"Either write me a cheque or give me information on Sparklefeet," Barbara whispered.

Gary sipped his tea as he shifted in his seat. "Dorian sent me an email this morning. He says we should pivot to mail orders and direct online sales, like a subscription service."

The manager returned to place a chicken salad in front

of Barbara. He stepped toward Rex, casting a shadow over him.

"Excuse me, but seats are for customers."

Rex's eyes darted between the Allens and the manager.

"Um, sorry. I am a customer?" Rex's voice rose as he spoke.

The manager leaned forward. "Are you sure?"

"Yes?"

"What did you buy?"

He pointed at Eddie. "My friend ordered me something."

To cover his face in a natural way, Eddie drank from the coffee. The drink filled his mouth as the manager stared. Eddie, hating the bitter taste, choked on the liquid and coughed up a small puddle. As he coughed, his round, hippy sunglasses slid down his nose.

The manager stood straight and tall. "You're barred!"

Eddie grimaced. "Sorry, what?"

The manager stomped across the aisle and knocked Eddie's hat off. "What's this? A disguise?"

He shoved Eddie into the drink fridge's new door.

Rex rose to his feet. "Hey, leave him alone."

The manager glared at Rex. "You're barred, too."

Gary and Barbara stared at Rex.

"What do you think you're doing?" Gary noticed the phone's display recording.

Rex smiled. "Um ... bye?"

The manager ripped the glasses from Eddie's face and crushed them in his hand.

"You want me to get my broom?"

"I'd rather you didn't," Eddie said as he backed away towards the front door.

Rex bolted down the aisle as Gary cut across the tables,

knocking over other people's food and drinks. Rex apologised to the customers as he passed by.

The manager stepped towards Eddie, who threw the half-full coffee cup at the manager's feet and ran out.

Gary lunged for Rex as he escaped out the front door.

ELEVEN

E ddie sprinted down the road. His belly throbbed, and his lungs shrank, but he didn't slow down until he turned into the side street where the Morris Minor was parked.

At the car, Eddie searched for Rex. He stared at the street corner, waiting. With his eyes on the corner, he unlocked the door, wondering if Gary had caught Rex and the phone.

Rex bounded into the side street. He rushed along the pavement with Gary behind him. Eddie got into the car, unlocked the passenger door, and attempted to start the engine. Flinging the door open, Rex plonked into the car seat.

Gary grabbed Rex's closing car door and yanked it wide open. Rex tried to dive for the back seat, but Gary grabbed his foot and pulled him out. He landed on the concrete and clawed at the car.

Eddie turned the key a third time, awakening the car's sputtery engine. He had his getaway, but not his partner or the recording.

Gary kicked Rex in the stomach. He let go of the car door and held his belly, curled up in the foetal position. In a frenzy, Gary reached into Rex's pockets until he pulled out the evidence.

"Ha!" Gary threw it on the ground and stomped it into pieces.

From the driver's seat, Eddie watched in horror. He certainly couldn't take on Gary—the man was a third larger than Eddie. The phone continued to break apart as Gary ground his heel into the small pile of plastic and metal.

As Gary gave Rex another kick, this time in the lower back, Rex popped his head out from the ball-shape he'd held himself in and smiled at Eddie.

Why's he smiling? Eddie thought. *He's getting beat up.*

Rex's eyes darted to the car's back seat. Eddie swung around. On the carpet behind the passenger seat, he spotted the phone, which must have fallen out when Rex was pulled out of the car.

Confused, Eddie leaned towards the passenger door to see the pavement. Gary stomped down, smashing up a black device, the same colour as Eddie's broken old pager. Rex switched them to trick Gary.

Eddie grabbed the phone and placed it in his coat pocket, brushing the play button.

"Dorian sent me an email this morning," Gary's voice said from the phone's speaker.

Gary stopped smashing the device and eyeballed Eddie.

Rex gave Eddie a thumbs-up. Eddie buckled his seatbelt and drove the Morris Minor off towards Sparklefeet Industries. The open passenger door hit a lamp post as he pulled forward. The impact dislodged the door and shoved it almost closed. Hanging an inch lower, the door swayed to and fro as the Morris Minor sped away.

As Eddie made his getaway, Rex blocked Gary by reaching his arms out wide. Gary kicked at Rex, but Rex grabbed the man's leg and hugged it tightly. Having failed to shake Rex off, Gary grabbed Rex by his corduroy jacket, lifted, and threw him against the wonky brick wall.

Rex flinched, expecting the decrepit wall to tumble down. After a few seconds of nothing, he drew a sigh of relief.

Gary sprinted towards the Morris Minor while Eddie slowed at a stop sign. Another car dawdled along the crossing street as Gary's reflection grew bigger in the rear-view mirror.

"Come on, come on," Eddie muttered.

The other car crossed the junction as Gary grabbed the Morris Minor's back door handle. Eddie put his foot on the accelerator. The door handle slipped out of Gary's grip.

The Morris Minor rumbled into the main road, creating some distance from Gary, who ran past the café towards the office building.

Eddie reached the barriers to the office car park. He pulled up to the ticket machine and vigorously rolled down his window with the hand crank. With the window a third of the way open, the hand crank popped off the door. The panicking detective fidgeted to get the hand crank back on. Through the wing-mirror, he saw Gary was a few buildings away and gaining.

Tired of the handle antics, Eddie squeezed his arm through the gap in the window and reached out. His fingers barely reached the ticket, but he squeezed even harder. He clamped the ticket between his fingernails and pulled the paper out.

The barrier raised as Eddie pulled his arm back in the car. He accelerated and parked in the visitor parking space, close to the front door.

As he dashed up the steps, he saw the Morris Minor was parked over the line, intruding on a second parking spot. Because it was in his nature to be a conscientious parker, he paused halfway up the steps, torn between the front door and the car. Across the car park, Gary ran past the barriers. Eddie gulped and bolted into the reception.

The security guard, alerted to Eddie's presence on the security monitors, stood in front of the elevator lobby, waving his arms and shaking his head.

"You're not allowed in the building," he said with an apologetic tone.

Eddie attempted to run around him. The guard pushed Eddie back.

"I need to see Dorian West now."

"If you get past me, then I'm fired. I'm already in trouble for threatening to pepper spray a tenant's nephew."

"That's Dorian, he'll want to know about this."

He pointed to the front door. "Get out."

Eddie faked to the right to throw off the guard, then ran to the left.

The security guard grabbed Eddie, twisted his arm, and dragged him back outside. Eddie tried to escape, but his slender frame was anchored by the heavy guard's grip. He opened the door by shoving Eddie against it. His cheek, shoulder, and left knee all knocked against the glass.

Outside, the guard let go of Eddie, dropping him to the concrete pathway at the top of the steps.

"Sorry," the guard said as he re-entered the building.

Gary hurried across the car park. A leaving vehicle braked to avoid hitting him.

Eddie scrambled back to his feet as Gary rushed up the steps. The panicking detective ran along the path toward the corner of the office building, right by the river's edge, hoping to escape down the side of the tower. At the corner, he found a six-foot metal fence with spikes on the top blocking the side access.

Cornered, Eddie peeked over the four-foot concrete wall bordering the muddy river. The water splashed against the marsh, ten feet below. Gary had slowed his approach, safe in the knowledge Eddie was trapped.

After offering a knowing smile, Gary hurtled towards Eddie. Although Eddie could run back into the car park, he knew each step was further away from Dorian, and he'd eventually get caught by Gary. If he wanted to succeed, he had to climb the fence. Eddie grabbed the fence's metal posts to support him and swung his feet to the top of the concrete river wall.

Teetering on the wall's edge, Eddie glimpsed below and grew light-headed. The rising tide enveloped a half-sunken shopping trolley stuck in the salty wetland. The water trickled around the jagged cans and broken bottles embedded in the marsh.

Eddie's mind raced through a series of worst-case scenarios. If he fell, he'd probably cut himself with the sharp edges of the broken bottles. Or if he landed on his back, the suction of the marsh would trap him as the tide came in. Or both, then he'd have to wait and see if he bled out or drowned first. With Gary as the only witness, it was unlikely the emergency services would be called.

As Gary stormed towards the wall, Eddie snapped out of his grim fantasy and lifted himself up the metal fence. His feet stood between the gaps of the fence spikes. For support, Eddie clung to the building wall by cramming his fingertips into the mortar gap between the yellow bricks.

Imagining a new worst-case scenario of impaling himself almost cost Eddie his balance. Past the fence, along the side of the building, a few scattered wooden crates looked like they could break his fall.

In the distance, Rex ran along the street towards the car park barriers. He waved both his hands and cheered Eddie on.

Gary ran along the walkway, seconds away from grabbing Eddie.

Eddie took a deep breath and jumped at the crates. Suspended in mid-air, Eddie stopped. As he dangled from the fence, he looked up over his shoulder. A spike had slid between his jacket and shirt, pinning him to the fence.

Trapped, he wiggled to loosen himself. After a few shuffles, the spike speared through the jacket. The sleeves rode up into his armpits. He was definitely stuck.

Gary reached the fence and grabbed Eddie by the hair.

"You give me that phone now."

Eddie kicked away from the fence until the tear in the jacket ripped down into the shoulders, loosening his left sleeve. He pulled his arm through the sleeve and pushed away from the fence.

Although he was released from the jacket, his scalp felt raw as he pulled his hair from Gary's grip. He landed on the wooden crates and rolled to face the fence.

Gary shouted and swore, shaking his clenched fist with pieces of Eddie's hair between each digit.

Eddie scurried down the side of the office until he remembered the phone was in his inner jacket pocket. He spun around and darted towards the fence.

Confused, Gary stepped back, as if Eddie was going to run through the fence and bulldoze him. Eddie reached the jacket, stuffed his hand into the pockets, and rummaged around.

Gary realised Eddie was searching for the phone and attempted to pull the jacket between the metal pickets. As Eddie took the phone from the pocket, Gary grabbed Eddie's wrist through the fence posts.

Eddie tried to bat the fist away, but Gary grabbed the free hand as well. Both Eddie's wrists were shackled by Gary's large, clenched hands. Eddie held the phone tight in his right hand, and Gary dragged his hands to the fence.

"Drop the phone through the bars," he said.

Eddie shook his head.

Gary raised both arms, lifting Eddie a few inches off the ground.

"Do it now."

With Gary's grip tightening, Eddie's grasp on the phone weakened. If he dropped the phone, it would bounce off the concrete wall and fall into the river's marsh below.

"Fine," Gary said. "We'll do this the hard way."

He shoved Eddie towards the river. The phone now teetered between the fingers of Eddie's right hand over the concrete wall. Ten feet below, the tide consumed the marsh and splashed against the river wall.

"Drop it in the river."

Eddie shook his head.

Gary snarled his teeth. "Either the phone goes, or you go. Understand?"

The phone slid a little, only Eddie's ring and little finger gripped it.

Two skinny arms leapt around Gary's neck. As they tightened, Gary's eyes bulged, and he roared. Rex's face raised over Gary's shoulder.

"Hi, Eddie."

Gary let go of Eddie's empty hand to fight off Rex. Rex bit the giant man's ear. He squealed, releasing Eddie's other hand.

Eddie dropped to the crate below. Gary spun around until he shook Rex off. As Gary chased Rex through the car park, Eddie got to his feet and scurried through the side of the building towards the docking bay.

Exhausted, Eddie reached the back of the building. He stomped his weak legs up the steps of the dock bay door and entered the warehouse.

In a daze, he stumbled through rows of crates full of cleaning products into the path of the forklift truck. The truck hit the brakes and honked.

"Sorry," Eddie said, trying to find the energy to speak.

The forklift truck driver shouted at him in Polish. Eddie didn't understand, but assumed it meant something along the lines of, 'get out the way.'

He arched his back and took a breath. "Where's the door?"

The man continued to talk in Polish and waved him off towards the lobby door.

As the soap scent tickled Eddie's sinuses, he hobbled to the door and pushed. It was locked. He remembered he needed a keycard to get in.

"Excuse me," he shouted out to the forklift truck. When he turned around, the truck had gone, deep into the warehouse.

Eddie searched around for the forklift truck. Behind him, the keycard reader beeped, and the door opened. He lined up against the wall next to the door, hoping to sneak past the person entering.

Gary Allen stepped out of the doorway, holding a golf club. He blocked Eddie's only escape as he surveyed the warehouse. The door automatically closed behind him.

"I know you're in here," he muttered. "And you aren't getting out."

TWELVE

Flush against the warehouse wall, Eddie held his breath, hoping Gary would go off looking for him. Gary took a few steps forward, tightening his grip on the golf club. He slowly examined every corner of the warehouse, except right behind him.

Eddie stared at the keycard hanging from Gary's pocket. Could he grab it and swipe the door's card reader with enough time to escape? Slowly, he reached out towards the keycard.

"Achoo!" The soap smell caused Eddie to sneeze.

Gary spun around and raised the golf club. "Hand over the phone."

Eddie sidestepped away from Gary and the door. "Or what, you'll hit me with that skinny little golf club? What's that gonna do?"

Gary whacked the club against a wall lamp, shattering the glass. "It'll make a dent or two."

Eddie took another step back, bumping into a pallet of boxed shoe cleaner. With the phone held to his chest,

Eddie searched around, hoping the forklift driver would return. Above him, he spotted a security camera.

He waved at the camera, "Help me!"

Gary hit Eddie in the head with the golf club. Eddie felt the solid thump against his temple. He fell to the hard concrete floor, which knocked the back of his skull.

He grumbled as his vision darkened and focus blurred. His hand dropped to the ground. The phone laid next to his hand. His fingers stroked the phone, but Gary placed the head of the golf club in Eddie's palm and pushed down.

"Sorry," Gary said. "But you've got to hustle, you've got to climb if you want to reach the top."

As Eddie lay there, he saw a white mouse scuttle by, dragging a cleaning cloth in its mouth across the warehouse floor. The mouse disappeared into a hole in the wall with shredded fabric poking out.

The mouse is making a nest, Eddie thought. *That's who's stealing the cloth.*

Eddie let out a loud, short "Ha!" followed by a fit of giggles.

Gary picked up the phone. "What's so funny?"

Eddie's vision brightened and focused. "If you've got pests, we're the bests." He laughed louder.

"Maybe I hit you a little too hard."

Gary tapped through the phone's options and played back the most recent recording file. It was his and Barbara's incriminating conversation. His thumb tapped the screen again.

"Deleted."

Gary walked around to Eddie's head, one foot over each shoulder. He waved the club to and fro by Eddie's head, readying to take a shot.

As Gary swung the club up, the locked door flung

open. Rex and the security guard ran out and shoved Gary to the ground. The security guard tackled Gary and pulled his arm behind his back.

"Don't make me pepper spray you!" the guard yelled.

Rex stepped over Gary and the security guard as they wrestled. He picked up the phone.

"We did it," Rex said as he helped Eddie up into a seated position.

Eddie rubbed his forehead. "It's too late."

"Nonsense," Rex said. "We have the phone."

Gary rolled over, shoving the security guard to the side.

Rex ran to the closed door. Gary chased him with a clenched fist. He swung at Rex, who dropped and rolled.

Gary punched the door and screamed. "Ahhh!"

As Rex got back to his feet, the security guard chucked his keycard at Rex. He grabbed the card and slid it into the door's reader.

Gary reached for Rex. Eddie grabbed the golf club and whacked Gary in the knee. Rex escaped as the door closed.

While holding his knee, Gary searched through his pocket to get his keycard. He slid it through and yanked the door open.

Eddie held the golf club through the door to keep it ajar. He staggered through the door, steadying himself against the walls while using the club as a walking stick.

Rex reached the elevators and repeatedly pushed the call button. Gary, who blocked the stairwell to the Sparklefeet office, snarled as he limped towards Rex.

With neither elevator headed to the ground floor, Rex raced to the security guard's front desk. He grabbed the intercom, pushed the red button, and held the phone close to the microphone.

Rex tapped the phone's play button. Audio of Rex

enthusiastically singing the lyrics to *The Fresh Prince of Bel Air* broadcast to the whole building.

Eddie slapped his forehead with his palm and winced from touching the growing bump.

Rex grimaced and checked the phone.

Gary hobbled towards Rex with murder in his eyes.

"He deleted it," Eddie called out.

Rex clicked through the phone's menu and into the trash can folder. He found the most-recent recording and pressed play.

Barbara's voice blasted through the hall speakers: "Either write me a cheque or give me information on Sparklefeet."

"Dorian sent me an email this morning," Gary's voice echoed. "He says we should pivot to mail orders and direct online sales, like a subscription service."

Gary reached the desk. He grabbed Rex by the neck and pinned him to the wall.

"It's over," Eddie shouted. "We won."

"Gary, cut it out." At the building's entrance, Barbara entered. She put her hands on her hips.

"Yeah, Gary," Rex said, his voice constricted.

Gary's eyes narrowed, his face inches from Rex's.

"Please?" Rex asked.

The elevator pinged. The doors opened, and Dorian stepped out.

"What's happening?" Dorian asked.

"Gary's the leak," Eddie said. "You just heard a recording we made of him giving secrets to Barbara Allen."

"You're a liar!" Gary shouted.

"Give it a rest." Barbara barked. "Is this really worth beating up two idiots for? Unless you want to go to jail as well as get fired. You can be so unpredictable."

Gary let go of Rex and turned to Barbara. "You always said you wanted me to be more spontaneous?"

Barbara rolled her eyes.

Dorian marched to the security desk. He took the phone and played the recording of Barbara and Gary again.

"I never sent that email."

Eddie wobbled past the elevators, still in a bit of a daze. "We did. Kevin helped us. It was bait to set up Gary, and he fell for it."

"That's really clever," Dorian said. "You guys did it."

Rex and Eddie smiled. Eddie reached the reception desk and leaned on it for support.

Dorian smiled. "You got fired on purpose, didn't you? So Gary would let his guard down."

Eddie loosened his tie, tempted to lie. "Well…"

He turned to Rex whose head-bobbing developed into an unconfident nod.

Eddie threw his hands up. "All part of the service."

"Genius," Dorian said. "Great work, guys." Dorian looked Gary up and down. "Gary, you're fired."

A week later, after Rex and Eddie had time to heal from their wounds, the pair arrived at the Sparklefeet office to settle up.

Bessie greeted them with a genuine smile. "Hello, Dorian's ready to see you right away."

The pair were a little taken aback by her warmth. As they passed the row of cubicles, they noticed the employees had a spring in their step. There were also a couple of new hires working away.

"It seems a bit busier, here?" Eddie said.

117

Bessie nodded. "Oh, yes. We've had quite the week."

Francis passed by with colour in his cheeks. "Hi, boys. Would love to catch up but I'm going out for lunch."

"Francis looks well," Rex said.

Eddie raised his eyebrows. "Not on the packed lunches anymore?"

Francis laughed. "Now that the company's stock has skyrocketed, I'm saved. Paid off the car and restocked my savings. It's off to the Café de Paris for me."

Eddie caught up with Bessie. "The company's stock went up?"

Bessie gave a broad smile as she opened Dorian's office door.

Dorian waved his arms in the air. "Rex and Eddie, come and have a seat."

The two confused detectives lowered into the seats opposite Dorian.

"You guys look good. Still a little bruised, but good."

Eddie nodded. "We came to settle the bill."

"I've already written you a cheque. I heard Ash Haynes paid you as well, must be a good week for you."

"Kind of," Eddie said. "Ash paid us a grand up front, but that barely covers the damage to our car door."

Dorian handed them a cheque with a grin. "This should get you back in the black."

Eddie smiled. "Two grand!"

We're getting paid, Eddie thought. *Like professionals.*

Finally, Eddie felt like a real detective. Instead of his usual sinking feeling, a persistent dread, he now felt a wave of confidence. He took a deep, calm breath as he re-read the cheque.

"Wow," Rex said. "We're rich."

Dorian stood and offered his hand.

Rex shook with vigour. "If you ever need our help again, let us know."

Eddie gave a solid shake. "It's been a pleasure."

Dorian gestured to the door. "Let me see you to the lifts."

They followed him through the row of cubicles.

"I hear the company stock is doing well," Eddie inquired.

"Yeah, we made a few changes, and we've seen huge growth."

"What happened?" Rex asked.

"Direct sales and online marketing," Dorian said. "After Kevin sent your email, he decided to make an app allowing people to order the shoe cleaning kit from their home. Whipped it up in a few hours."

Eddie's eyes narrowed. "But he was fired for sexual harassment."

"He's freelance now, works from home. I decided to put the money we had left into online ads, and people signed up in droves. We are raking in the cash now."

As they reached the elevators, Dorian pushed the call button. "I figured, let Ash have the shopping centres, we're reaching people nationwide."

"That was my idea," Eddie said.

Dorian's brow wrinkled. "It was your idea to let Ash have the shopping centres?"

The elevator doors opened with a ping.

"No, it was my idea to do direct sales and online marketing. The app is my idea."

Dorian shook his head. "It was Kevin's idea to do the app."

Eddie stiffened. "What about the online marketing? I said that."

Dorian scoffed. "I did the online marketing."

He patted them on the back, guiding them into the elevator.

"So how much is Sparklefeet worth now?" Rex said.

"We've tripled in value. That's almost half a million in a week. Who knows where we will be by the end of the month?"

Eddie stared at the two grand cheque in his hand. Those four digits seemed tiny now.

Rex stopped the closing lift doors with his arm. "Do we still get our handsome bonus?"

"Oh, I forgot to mention it. Of course you do," Dorian said.

Eddie's eyes widened.

I saved Sparklefeet single-handedly, he thought. *What are we going to get? Another cheque? Shares in the company?*

Dorian smiled. "A lifetime supply of shoe cleaning kits. We shipped a pallet to your office, oh…" He checked his watch. "Half an hour ago."

"Wow," Rex said, excited. "A lifetime's supply, that's like, half a life each."

Eddie swallowed. "Perfect."

"Good work, guys." Dorian winked.

The elevator doors closed. As the lift went down, Eddie's sinking feeling returned.

Rex & Eddie return in

THE THIRD BANANA

GET A FREE BOOK!

One of the best things about writing is building a relationship with my readers. I occasionally send newsletters with details on new releases, special offers, and other news related to the Rex & Eddie Mysteries series.

When you sign up to my newsletter I'll send you ***Rebels Without A Claus: A Rex & Eddie Mystery***, a novelette set between book 1 and book 2!

Get your freebie today by signing up at

WWW.SEAN-CAMERON.COM/FREEBOOK

ENJOY THIS BOOK?
YOU CAN MAKE A BIG DIFFERENCE!

Book reviews are an excellent tool for getting the attention of new readers. If you've enjoyed *The Office Spy* I would be very grateful if you could spend just five minutes leaving an honest review (it can be as short as you like) on the book's Amazon page.

Thank you very much.

ABOUT THE AUTHOR

Sean Cameron is from Rochester, England and currently lives in Los Angeles, California. When not laughing at the British weather report, he finds time to write the comedy book series *Rex & Eddie Mysteries*.

He likes carrot cake, dinosaurs, and hiking; although not much hiking happens as he fears being eaten by a mountain lion. He dislikes squash soup, traffic, and mountain lions.

You can drop him an email at sean@sean-cameron.com or visit his online home at www.sean-cameron.com.

facebook.com/seancameronauthor

twitter.com/seancameronuk

instagram.com/seancameronuk

amazon.com/author/seancameron

ALSO BY SEAN CAMERON

Catchee Monkey: A Rex & Eddie Mystery (Book 1)

Amateur sleuths Rex and Eddie stumble upon a murder mystery that sees them outnumbered, outgunned, and outwitted. They'll have to solve the case before it kills them or before they end up killing each other. *Catchee Monkey* is a hilarious detective novella that's equal parts British Comedy and gripping thriller.

Feline Fatale: A Rex & Eddie Mystery (Book 2)

Rex and Eddie accept a case to find the missing cat of their old school teacher and first crush, Mrs Nerdlinger. The duo are pitted against a creepy stalker, a nosey neighbour, and a rude old woman claiming to be the cat's real owner. *Feline Fatale* is a fun and farcical thriller full of sharp dialogue, clever twists, and silly antics.

The Office Spy: A Rex & Eddie Mystery (Book 3)

Spies, sleuths, and sandwich thieves — For Rex and Eddie, it's just another day in the office. Hired to find a corporate spy, Rex and Eddie go undercover as pest exterminators. Their spy hunting antics entangle the pair in office politics, employee secrets, and the search for the kitchen's sandwich thief. *The Office Spy* is a fun novella packed with silly hijinks, clever jokes, and crazy thrills.

The Third Banana: A Rex & Eddie Mystery (Book 4)

After a routine surveillance job ends in witnessing a kidnapping, dimwitted detectives Rex and Eddie get on the wrong side of super sleuth Jason Cole. He's special forces, they're just… special. Now the detective duo must prove their worth against the best, solve the kidnapping case, and stop a gang turf war that could destroy their hometown. Full of witty mayhem, *The Third Banana* is a comedy thriller with appeal.

ACKNOWLEDGMENTS

I'd like to thank the following for their help with this book: Eleanor Hoal, Sam Whittam, Kristen Curran, and Aaron Orullian.

www.ingramcontent.com/pod-product-compliance
Lightning Source LLC
Chambersburg PA
CBHW052001170626
46808CB00007B/2722